D0177758

First published in 2018
by Currach Press
23 Merrion Square
Dublin 2, Ireland
www.currachbooks.com

Copyright © 2018 John Scally

ISBN: 978 1 78218 902 2

Set in Linux Libertine 12/16
Illustrations and cover design by Alba Esteban
Book design by Alba Esteban and Maria Soto | Currach Press
Printed by ScandBook, Sweden

BEAUTIFUL THOUGHTS FOR BEAUTIFUL MINDS

JOHN SCALLY

CURRACH
PRESS

To Luke Schmidt

Table of Contents

Foreword

By Miriam O'Callaghan

In my work on *Prime Time* I am exposed to all the troubles of the nation and the world. There are times when it seems like there is nothing but bad news. I am acutely aware of the many difficulties so many people face today.

In these troubled times we live in, it is nice to take time out to reflect on a project like this which focuses on 'Beautiful Thoughts for Beautiful Minds'.

There are 40,000 people in Ireland who have epilepsy, which is described as a group of long-term neurological disorders characterised by epileptic seizures. All royalties from this book go to Epilepsy Ireland. I am very happy to be associated with such a worthy cause.

I hope your beautiful minds will take inspiration and comfort from these beautiful thoughts.

Acknowledgements

I am deeply grateful to Joe Schmidt for his interest in this book and for his ongoing kindness.

I am profoundly thankful to Miriam O'Callaghan for honouring me by writing the foreword for this book.

Thanks also to Tony Ward for his generosity.

Thanks to Garry O'Sullivan, Mags Gargan and all at Currach Press for their support of this project.

Thanks to Michael Carty, Conor Culkin and all at Epilepsy Ireland for their enthusiasm for this fundraiser.

As always I am very thankful to my good friend John Littleton for his enduring goodness and for his practical help with this venture.

Catherine Defaux has been a beacon of love and courage while this book was being written.

Emilie Mazzucato was much in my thoughts and I am always impressed by her rich vein of goodness.

Lydia Greene has shown great grace in the face of adversity.

We lost the much loved Maisie Maher as this book was completed. May she rest in peace.

In May we lost Josephine Cregan who will be much missed by her devoted son Michael and all her loving children and grandchildren.

Maggie Burns is always an embodiment of beautiful thoughts in beautiful minds.

My gratitude to Mia McAleese whose love for her beloved sister Rosanna brought a tear to my eye because of its breathtaking beauty.

Trish O'Brien is the living witness of her own beautiful thought: "May the dreams you hold dearest be those which come true and kindness you spread keep returning to you."

Sarah Redmond is a human incarnation of Mark Twain's idea that: "Kindness is the language that the blind can see and that the deaf can hear."

My great gratitude to Patricia Seery, a woman of amazing grace.

Like Elizabeth and Jane Bennett, Lisa and Katy Dobey were married in quick succession this year. It is a truth universally acknowledged that they both deserve great happiness. Likewise I hope Danielle Lawless will discover that love is all around.

Judith McAdam's star has shone brightly this year. May it always be thus.

Introduction

Growing up on a small farm in Roscommon I never failed to get a little thrill from bringing a lamb into the world, especially after a very difficult birth. I felt I was part in some small way of achieving the miracle of new life. It would be melodramatic to say it was a religious experience but a warmth flowed through my body like a sliding, sun-dappled river. The birth was a language of hope, lyrical yet maddeningly inarticulate, alive to the resonances of everyday life. The first sound of the breathing of the new lamb was the breathing of hope.

Once I witnessed the dawn breaking as I went out to check on sickly lamb. I woke early, long before the first faint vestiges of light illuminated the specklings of frost on the hard ground. Despite my haste, as I pulled back the curtains I was compelled to watch the world take shape. Sunrise so rose my spirits that I could later easily understand why dawn worship had been a powerful article of belief for the pagan Celts.

A tumult of sound greeted me, every bird in the fields singing its heart out, although it was still dark. Gradually the sky lightened and the low, bruised clouds began to be caressed with red. The faint horizontal threads of clouds were growing a fiercer red against the still grey sky, the streaks intensified to scarlet and to orange and to gold, until the whole sky was a breath-taking symphony of colour. Then for a few moments as the dawn broke the birds fell silent. The carollers drew close and paused to seek out instruments, searching for the string, the bow, the drum, to make the appropriate melody. That was the instant the sun appeared over the horizon. The birds went silent because of the wonder, and that was the only possible response. Praise was secondary. It seemed that all of nature was affected by a tremor of excitement, adoring the creator. Timelessness breathed through the daybreak like the heartbeat of a new baby. When the birds began to sing again, it was not the pre-dawn chorus at all but something more reverential, like a heavenly choir. Subtle tunes resonated with ancient harmonies. It was like the first music ever made. All life was simplified. All thoughts were complete. Music was the best for this. The words of everyday are unworthy vehicles to describe the transcendent. This was theological reflection at its most eloquent.

I love to be inspired by nature, people and by beautiful thoughts. I also love people who have that wonderful capacity to make me smile - even just a little. In marked contrast when I watch the news on television or read newspapers I generally feel depressed. We live in troubled times, in a world that often seems worried and weary. Increasingly it seems that there is a diminishing place for the good, the glad and the beautiful.

In thinking of ways to fundraise for Epilepsy Ireland, the idea for a collection of beautiful thoughts for beautiful minds was born. This book is a unique amalgam of fact and fiction, authentic and autobiographical, humour and humanity. Some names have been changed – generally to protect the guilty! I hope you will enjoy it.

SECTION A:

THE GOOD, THE GLAD AND THE BEAUTIFUL

1

Magic Moments

In the rich architecture of our lives there are always people who leave an indelible mark on us and who shape our values and vision. They nurture our sense of right and wrong, inform our thoughts and feelings, and dictate the people we become. In this very personal chapter I reflect on some of the beautiful thoughts that have come my way and a few of the more comic moments.

In the name of the Grandfather

My drowsy eyes suddenly explode into life as I scan my new copy of *The Roscommon Herald* at the sight of a black and white photograph of an old man and a young boy patting a horse in a mud-splaterred field.

The picture is like a pandora's box, which opens a cascade of emotions within me. Despite my best efforts to the contrary, tears blur my vision and topple in steady streams along my cheeks. In that moment I am transported to another time and place.

On the last Saturday of October my father died. He was 35 years old. Looking back now I mourn for the unfinished business between us - so many things that I would have liked to say but never got the chance.

When my father died my grandfather became possibly the most important person in my life. I was called after him. Even his birthday was the same as mine.

Although I was physically like my father I inherited many of my grandfather's characteristics and qualities. The gap of two generations between us did not seem to matter. Whenever it was necessary he had no hesitation in bringing me down a peg or two, but criticism was always tactfully offered. In the cossetted comfort of his presence I learned much about patience, kindness and selflessness.

Part of my world collapsed on that May day when I heard that he died.

His funeral will live with me forever - looking down on a gathering for an occasion almost unbearably sad; a centre of my life gone. I was near to tears and in my heart there was something breaking. I hoped fervently that he would find peace at last in a higher, more perfect world. Today when I look in the mirror it is his face that looks back at me.

I loved being with him on the rare occasions he was working with the horse. I was enthralled by the magnificence of the animal, noble, imperious, majestic, powerful. Yet my abiding image of my grandfather is with his donkey and cart. The donkey knew the fields so well that there was no need to steer. The only flaw in his make-up was that he had a fear of water, arising from the fact that he had fallen into a bog hole in his youth.

If there was one reason why I loved my grandfather so much, it was that he always listened to me. He never cut me off in mid-stream. I always felt that he valued my opinion, even when my ideas were totally harebrained. I was deeply grateful that he was living with us otherwise I would just have been a 'Mammy's boy', without a dominant male in my life.

Although breakfast on Sunday morning was conducted in semi-silence in deference to Ciaran MacMathuna's music show on RTÉ radio, my grandfather's favourite music was birds singing. He especially loved the cuckoo, which sent its voice of mystery from out the woodland depths and wide-open spaces calling nature to rejoice at the advent of spring.

The song of the cuckoo was an echo of the halcyon days in paradise, rendering nature what it truly is: beautiful, poetic life at its innocent best, the world as it ought to be, the ideal for a moment realised. As we took refuge in a canopy of trees during April showers everything seemed made from memory. The sound of the cuckoo enshrouded us with a redemptive feeling, melting away depression, pain and bitter disappointment. Her dulcet tones hinted at a bygone age of innocence and values that no longer exist. The music was sweet and sensual, evocative of a higher world.

With EEC membership [now EU], the point of demarcation between farming and commerce became harder to identify. These changes were not all to our advantage. One of the unforeseen consequences was that the sounds changed. I always loved spending a warm June evening, milk can in hand, listening to the warm milk squirting into the pail as I milked the cows. Most of the animals were docile creatures. They allowed me to crouch on the stool and with my head against their flanks to effortlessly send a white milky jet hissing and frothing into the bucket. Soon that music was replaced by the dull droning of the plague of clinical, time-efficient milking machines that infested the area.

From my grandfather's point of view, the most disappointing feature of the change of landscape was the virtual disappearance of the corncrake. They were the victims of progress; when silage came in their natural habitat was destroyed. It was my father who first introduced me to the sweet sound of the corncrake. Once we had gone out in the still night to check a newly-born calf, we drank together from the bird's symphony of raucous notes pleading in the night. He seemed to bring out not just good tidings but elation. I always associated that

sound with sun drenched summers in the age of my innocence before my father died.

Memory is blurred and softened by time but I always
remember those summers as times of perpetual sunshine,
bright moonscapes and the sound of laughter. I wondered
if the corncrake suffered from insomnia; he always seemed
to be in full voice just as everyone else was trying to sleep.
I often cursed the age of silage for depriving me not just of
the corncrake but of all the nostalgia, the wide-eyed simplicity and the unadulterated happiness and excitement.

Some of my friends at school spent their evenings
stealing birds eggs and vandalising nests. My grandfather
made me solemnly swear that I would not partake of such
activities. He saw it as a crime against nature, psycholog-
ically and spiritually unhealthy, claiming: "Every time we
kill something; something inside us dies too."

One Man and his Horse

In our village a man's character was measured by his relationship with his horse. When I was a boy I loved listening to my grandfather because his stories were so full of warmth and unfinished sentences of mystery and hope. In particular I loved when he talked about horses because of his almost obsessive's passion.

One day walking in the fields with him lives in my memory. It was the ploughing. The horse needed the minimum of direction, as if on automatic pilot. The curve-sided plough smoothly and tenderly penetrated the skin of the earth, throwing the sod sweetly to the right of the mow and then crashing onto a big stone and the clash making an annoying sound. The horse made his own music with his panted breathing and occasional snorting. It was rough ground and very hard on my little legs. It was with great relief that I saw the last sod was turned.

Country people see this time of the year in a gentle light. There was plenty of fresh air about on that unseasonally cold, grey day. The lake was a mirror to the clouds. We walked gingerly towards a hedge where I had recently spotted a group of pheasants. The hedge was empty, though a gang of geese were stamping their webbed feet nearby in hopes of scraps. Suddenly I let out a cry of horror.

"What's wrong pet?" asked my grandfather in a voice full of concern.

I had spotted a rabbit with its leg caught in a snare. She was alive but whimpering, terrified. Her eyes were deep pools of pain. The snare had dug deep. My grandfather delicately held the creature with one hand and tried to loosen the snare with the other. He whispered softly to the rabbit, tenderly telling him he was only trying to help. But he knew from the way it squirmed that the rabbit couldn't separate the pain of the snare from his efforts to free it. It was an intimate moment, a primitive communion with a desperate creature who needed a friend. With each convulsion the snare bit deeper.

After much wailing from me my grandfather finally got the snare wire off the leg. At first the rabbit just remained shivering. Then it realised it was liberated and fled, bruised but free. My grandfather pulled up the peg that held the snare and flung it into the lake nearby.

The memory of the rabbit's fierce struggle with the snare has remained with me as a metaphor for the human capacity to inflict pain and suffering onto itself.

The Faithful Departed

The richly carpeted room was unlike anything I had ever seen. Beautiful antiques were placed all around it. In the centre was an ornately carved table, and the walls were covered in murals, conspicuous among them one of Noah's Ark. It was strange that my first visit to the canon's parlour was the day of his funeral. I was almost overcome with grief, not because of the occasion but because I had been told my services weren't needed as an altar-boy. A pound note gone down the drain.

The canon's funeral Mass was an awesome, if chaotic sight. The spectacle of a bishop and a multitude of priests, crammed together like bees in a hive behind the altar, made a lasting impression on the faithful. Never have so few stood somewhere so little for so long. One of the priests had forgotten his vestments. As he was only five-foot-one, an old, frilly white alb was found for him. He looked like a cross between an altar boy and Tom Thumb.

The first problem was caused by the microphone. It seemed to have taken on a life of its own and emitted various crackling sounds at the most solemn moments. Such was the disturbance that one of the priests turned it off. This brought hazards of its own. The celebrants had to rely on vocal projection. While this was fine for the bishop, it was less so for Monsignor Rodgers, who always spoke as if he was suffering from a bout of tonsillitis. Those priests whose vocal ranges were somewhere in between seemed to think that they were obliged to break the sound barrier by shouting, rather than reciting, their modest contribution to the liturgical celebration.

The second problem was that everybody assumed that somebody else was organising the ceremony, so nobody knew who was doing what or what was supposed to be happening. A priest would stand up to intone some prayer and just as abruptly sit down on discovering that at least one other colleague had beaten him to it. There were protracted pauses as everybody looked to the bishop to see what would happen.

Of course there was the choir. For reasons best known to himself, the late canon had taken a particular aversion to the choir, with the result that they were normally only to be heard on Midnight Mass and Christmas Day. In the light of the musical talent which was evident on those occasions, the canon's decision to employ their services so sparingly looked more and more judicious. Neither the organ nor the organist were in the first flush of youth nor even in the second. The combination of two idiosyncratic performances made for interesting - if not elegant - listening. The choir predictably lived down to expectations. Even by their own standards they were abysmal. The problem was exacerbated by the fact that the assembled clergy seemed to have formed a rival choral group, apparently singing the same hymns at a different speed to a different arrangement and musical notation.

The last straw was the prayers of the faithful, which Monsignor Rodgers had arranged beforehand. Gerry 'The Hop' McCarthy, the canon's right hand man in the parish, had been asked to say one of the prayers as a recognition of his loyal service and friendship to our late pastor. In a trembling voice he mumbled something indistinguishable, even to those in the front row. He gained confidence however with each word - only to make an embarrassing *faux pas* just when his voice was clearly audible - by praying for the canon's 'immorality' rather than 'immortality'.

The Blow-In

My grandfather was always suspicious about blow-ins. I suspected that his hostility was fuelled by his animosity for our next-door neighbour, twice removed, Mary Murphy. If gossip had been electricity, she would have been a power station. Given the poison that emanated from her tongue, my grandfather referred to her in private as Atilla the Hen.

For some reason though he got on famously with Frankie Walsh, who had moved down south after he inherited his late uncle's farm. Frankie's strong Tyrone accent gave him an exotic quality. Despite the best efforts of Father Time, his 63-year-old face was still exquisitely handsome. His features were flawlessly chiselled: his grey hair tinged with flecks of ginger, his skin smooth and hinting of a tan.

He was tall, with long, bony extremities and a strangely disproportionate round belly. His dark green eyes were unreadable or shyly sensitive depending on whether you took the trouble to get to know him or not.

His house was spartan-like in its frugality. The only exception was the parlour, a honeycomb of boxes filled with gramophone records. Pride of place was reserved for Delia Murphy's 'Spinning Wheel'. The green tile floor in the kitchen always looked dusty no matter how often it was swept.

Frankie was responsible for broadening my vocabulary. It was he who introduced me to a new phrase, 'jumping the border'. I thought this sounded like a great craic and I immediately requested a trip up north to take part in this athletic activity. It took a lot of patient work to explain to me that this was a code name for smuggling.

Every Sunday afternoon Frankie regaled my grandfather and I with stories about his dealings with the customs officers. The fabric of trust was forever torn between him and these men following an incident involving the movement of a large number of cattle over the border in the middle of night. Frankie always claimed that the episode was a "simple misunderstanding". As a result he was searched every day as he cycled home from his workplace - a poultry factory in Monaghan.

Frankie's eyes twinkled mischievously as he filled us in on his plan to pay back the customs officers. On the back of his bicycle he always carried a cardboard box full of stones and on front he carried a grocery bag full of little sticks. Exhaustive searches never uncovered any contraband.

After what seemed an eternity my grandfather asked the question that was burning on my lips, "So what exactly were you smuggling?"

Frankie paused dramatically before giving a one word answer – "Bicycles!"

A Teacher to Remember

The afternoon remained beautifully raw, with a flawless blue sky offering sunlight as pale as malt whisky - though much less warming. As she rang the bell to summon us back into class, Mrs Kelly's lilac corduroys and clumpy shoes made a bold fashion statement. She normally wore an ensemble that could have been looted from a jumble sale by someone with a severe visual impairment. The wind, having tried unsuccessfully to scrape the light make-up from her blue-green eyes, concentrated on blowing the short brown hair into thick bunches about a face that mirrored the liveliness and contained strength of her nature. She was small, but not at all frail, with square, capable hands adorned with a wedding ring as broad as a bangle.

Inside the cramped classroom, anticipation mingled with apprehension as she stated that she had an announcement for us. A lengthy theatrical pause ensued as she sat in an ordinary armchair which enclosed her like a small cave. Mrs Kelly's statements were sometimes as enigmatic as the Dead Sea Scrolls. A chorus of groans greeted the news that we were to have our annual visit from the community doctor. A large frown crossed Mrs Kelly's forehead. Her demeanour was almost always friendly to the point of fervour, but in rare moments, especially if she suspected she was being taken for less than she was, a glacial sternness came over her features and only the resolute hung around to debate. Then her thick-lensed glasses steamed up as she wagged her finger. All thoughts of dissent were suspended and we meekly responded as one, "Yes Miss." The width of her smile echoed the generosity of her nature.

Privately we were aghast. Dr Stewart was a short, stocky man whose pugnacious features and brisk, assertive gestures might mark him as a former professional boxer. He usually looked about as cheerful as a man trying to get a cyanide capsule out from behind his teeth. When he formed a set of opinions he was slow to rearrange them. He was to visit us to check our eyesight and hearing.

Almost as one we turned around to look at Stephen. His thin-framed glasses under high waves of strawberry-blonde hair partially concealed his shrewd, rather pouchy face. Nonetheless it was clear that his normally boyishly pleasant expression was a study in anxiety.

Stephen had been in a car accident six months previously. His face had been disfigured, though the scars were fading. Looking back into the blank spaces of memory, we were unpardonably cruel in the comments we made about them. Stephen's self-confidence had taken a battering. He also suffered from intermittent hearing loss.

Mrs Kelly decided to give all of our hearing a little test. She asked us individually to put our right hand up to our right ear and to repeat back a sentence she dictated to us. There was a collective intake of breath when it came to Stephen's turn.

He was obsessed with butterflies. The fascination arrived like talking, too early to remember. I would have bet my last thrupenny bit that Mrs Kelly would have asked him something about butterflies - but not for the first time our teacher fanned the flames of imagination and surprised me.

Stephen's face lightened like a cloudless dawn as he confidently repeated Mrs Kelly's sentence, "I wish you were my little boy".

Power to the People

A good sprinkling of politicians were in attendance when I went to the funeral of a distant relative recently. One of their number strode towards me with an air of purpose. To date his biggest political achievement has been his own advancement. He is in his early forties, but trying to ignore the passage of time; young hair-style, young dress, young affectation of speech. His voice had the faintest of lisps as he talked with animation, the veins in his neck turning a deep shade of red. The big man paused before me and knitted his brow, as though puzzled, before finding his second breath. His mouth opened like a landed fish and when he eventually spoke the words had no impact. He offered me his sincere sympathy but his roaming eyes said otherwise.

Suddenly I was entangled in the clinging cobwebs of childhood and I recalled the first politician I knew - the late Seamus O'Malley. Seamus was a legend in his own lifetime, at least in his own mind. As was often the custom in old style Irish politics, he had inherited the seat on the county council from his father. He was the opposite of everything expected of a politician: physically bulky, almost obese, intellectually backward and with apparently no understanding of the social graces. If he had been at the Last Supper he would have insisted that they eat bacon and cabbage. He had an uncanny ability to turn ordinary situations into moments of excruciating embarrassment. Yet he was a phenomenal vote-getter because in spite of ourselves, we all liked him.

He travelled the funeral circuit assiduously, made a point of speaking at every county council meeting where there was a reporter present and always said what he thought people wanted to hear, even if he had said the exact opposite a day or even ten minutes earlier.

He was never too bothered about ideology. I always suspected that he thought the swing to the left was the sharp turn after Joey McManus' hayshed.

In the light of his tendency to say and do extraordinary things, most of them by accident, he had acquired the reputation of being fearless. This was not the case. He had one great fear, his older sister Mary, a nun, who was the mother superior in the local convent. She had intelligent green eyes and a mischievous smile.

Her most upsetting quality was that she continually transgressed what our culture has defined as a socially acceptable distance between two people when they were standing in conversation. She stood up right beside you and confronted you with her intense facial expression and penetrating stare. Men, in particular, found this unnerving and normally tried to back away, often ending up literally with their backs to the wall, as she followed in close pursuit.

Seamus was far from being politically correct. His hobby was shooting rabbits. One day, back in a rare fine summer, he visited our neighbour on a hunting expedition. He left his gun on the rocking chair, much to Mrs Brady's chagrin. She was tending to stoutness, although there was strength and determination in her stern features. Her gait was stiff, her skin was papery, and there was a pallor about her that was indicative of a recent illness. She inquired:

"Is that thing loaded?"

"No Nancy. At least I don't think so. Let me just check for you."

Rather than doing the obvious thing and checking for bullets, Seamus pointed the gun towards the front window and pulled the trigger.

A shattering sound and hysterical screaming followed. Seamus calmly stated:

"Sorry Nancy. Be Gawd it must have been loaded after all."

The Good One

The times are changing. I was thinking of that the other day when I went into a shop and a little girl and her mother were shopping. The lady behind the counter gave the little girl a bar of chocolate. "What do you say, Kylie?" asked her mother. Young Kylie said: "Charge it!"

I grew up in rural Ireland as the era of 'the rambling house' was coming to an end. The undisputed star of that epoch was someone who could tell 'a good one' – a little story that gave you food for thought or else could make you smile. The best ones are those that linger long in the memory. These are some of the 'good ones' I recall from my childhood.

Persistence

It is said that courage is not the absence of fear, but rather the judgement that something else is more important than fear. If we turn away from a challenge once, it is so much easier to do the same again the next time, and the next. Showing some courage in less serious difficulties is often the best training for the major crises. Courage is like a muscle. It is strengthened with use.

Once upon a time there was a young prince who was meandering around distant lands looking for adventure. He came to a town which was near a pass into a fertile valley. The prince was taken aback by the poverty in the town and inquired why the people did not move into the valley. The locals told him that they couldn't because a dragon was guarding the pass and that they were all afraid of him. As princes so often do in stories like this, the prince decided that he was going to solve the problem irrespective of his own personal safety.

The next day was cold, wet and windy. He woke long before dawn, dragged from sleep by rain pounding on the roof. The atmosphere outside was menacing, and a steadily strengthening wind did nothing to help. It made the trees roar, and it whistled through the gravestones, an agitated, unsettling sound that made the robin on his windowsill more jittery.

With a brave smile but with a knot in his stomach, the prince made his way to the pass. With his sword waving he reached his destination. To his great surprise all he could see was a tiny little dragon, who was only the size of his boot.

"Where's your father?" asked the prince. The dragon said, "I live here on my own."

"But how can a tiny little beast like you so terrify the local people?"

"Because of my name."

"What's your name?"

"What Might Happen?"

From a distance, what might happen is a terrifying prospect but by having the courage to confront the dragons we learn that we may be better able to cope with them than we could ever have imagined.

A Broken Friendship
(African folk tale)

Frissie the Frog and Slimy Shady the Snake met as strangers in the forest one day, and played together all day.

"Watch what I can do," said Frissie the Frog, and he hopped high into the air. "I'll teach you if you want," he offered.

So he taught Slimy Shady how to hop, and together they hopped up and down the path through the forest.

"Now watch what I can do," said Slimy Shady, and he crawled on his belly straight up the trunk of a tall tree. "I'll teach you if you want."

So he taught Frissie how to slide on his belly and climb trees.

After a while they both grew hungry and decided to go home for lunch, but they promised to meet each other the next day.

"Thanks for teaching me how to hop," said Slimy Shady.

"Thanks for teaching me how to crawl up trees," said Frissie.

Then they each went home.

"Look what I can do, mother," cried Frissie, crawling on his belly.

"Where did you learn how to do that?" his mother asked.

"Slimy Shady the Snake taught me," he answered. "We played together in the forest this morning, he's my new friend."

"Don't you know that the Snake family is a bad family?" his mother asked. "They have poison in their teeth. Don't ever let me see you crawling on your belly either. It isn't proper."

Meanwhile Slimy Shady went home and hopped up and down for his mother to see.

"Who taught you to do that?" she asked.

"Frissie Frog," he said, "he's my new friend."

"What foolishness," said his mother. "Don't you know that we've been on bad terms with the Frog family for longer than we can remember. The next time you play with the frog, catch him and eat him up. And stop that hopping. It isn't our custom."

So next morning when Frissie met Slimy Shady in the forest, he kept his distance.

"I'm afraid I can't go crawling with you today," he called, hopping back a hop or two.

Slimy Shady eyed him quietly, remembering what his mother had told him. "If he gets too close, I'll spring at him and eat him," he thought.

But then he remembered how much fun they had together, and how nice Frissie had been to teach him how to hop. So he sighed sadly to himself and slid away into the bush. And from that day on, Frissie and Slimy Shady never played together again. But they often sat alone in the sun, each thinking about their one day of friendship.

Words to the Wise

The Buddha was sitting by the side of the road when a traveller came along. The traveller stopped and said, "I'm on my way to the big city. Tell me what the people are like there."

The Buddha replied, "You tell me first where you're from and what the people are like there, and I'll tell you what they are like in the city."

Quick as a flash the traveller responded, "I come from the tiny town of Hamleta and they are all cheats and liars."

The Buddha sighed sadly and said, "Alas those are exactly the same sort of people you'll find in the big city."

Not long after a second traveller came along the road. He also said to the Buddha, "I'm on my way to the big city. Tell me what the people are like there."

The Buddha replied, "You tell me first where you're from and what the people are like there, and I'll tell you what they are like in the city."

The second journeyman responded, "I come from the tiny town of Hamleta and they are all honest and honourable people."

The Buddha beamed a wonderful smile and replied, "Good news my friend, those are exactly the same sort of people you'll find in the big city."

With a little help from my friends

One day a magnificent lion lay asleep in the sunshine. A little mouse ran across his paw and woke him up. The lion was furious and was going to eat him up when the little mouse cried, "Oh please let me go, sir. Some day I may help you."

The lion laughed at the idea that the little mouse could be of any use to him. But he was a good natured lion, and he set the mouse free. Not long after, the lion got caught in a net. He tugged and pulled with all his might, but the ropes were too strong. Then he roared loudly. The little mouse heard him and he ran to the spot. He said, "Be still, dear lion, and I will set you free. I will break these ropes." With his sharp little teeth, the mouse cut the ropes, and the lion came out of the net.

"You laughed at me once," said the mouse. "You thought I was too little to do you a good turn. But see, you owe your life to a poor little mouse."

Water, water everywhere

A very religious woman was at home when a storm came and the river burst its banks. Soon the water was up to the level of the first storey of her house. A man passed by her house in a raft and offered to take her to safety. She said, "No. Allah will save me."

As the water continued to rise the woman waited in her upstairs bedroom. A man rowed by her window in a boat. He stopped and offered to rescue her. She replied, "No thank you. Allah will save me."

The water rose higher and higher. The woman had to climb on her roof to stay alive. A helicopter passed by and offered to rescue her. The woman shouted, "No, Allah will save me."

The rain got heavier and heavier and the water got higher and higher. An hour later the woman drowned.

Sometime later the woman's spirit met with Allah in the next world. She was very angry and shouted at him, "Why did you not save me during the flood? I trusted you. I was sure you would come to my assistance."

Allah calmly replied, "I sent you a raft, a boat and a helicopter."

Copycats

....

David Darcy had one big problem. He wanted to be like Gerry Peters but Gerry didn't like him. David walked like Gerry walked; he talked like Gerry talked.

Then one day Gerry started to change. He began to hang around with Paul Mathews. He walked like Paul; he talked like Paul. And then it dawned on David that Paul Matthews walked and talked like Barry Butler. And Barry Butler walked and talked like Vernon Vincent.

So here David is, walking and talking like Gerry Peters' imitation of Paul Matthews version of Barry Butler trying to walk and talk like Vernon Vincent.

And who do you think Vernon Vincent is always walking and talking like? Of all people, dopey Terry Treacy - that little pest who walks and talks like David Darcy.

Please, Please Me

There was once a little word named 'Please'. It lived in a girl's mouth called Jane. Pleases live in everybody's mouth, though a lot of people forget they are there. All Pleases like to be taken out of people's mouths from time to time, just to feel that they are alive.

The Please who lived in Jane's mouth seldom got the chance to get out, because Jane was a very bold and rude girl. She almost never said 'Please'.

Whenever she needed something she just said: "Give me sweets. Give me chocolate."

Her parents didn't like this because they were very polite. Jane's poor Please was in awful state because it was sitting up in the roof of Jane's mouth without ever getting any use. It was growing weaker day by day.

Jane had a sister called Linda. Linda was Jane's older sister and a very nice, polite girl. Her Please was very happy because Linda used her all the time.

One day at breakfast, Jane's Please felt that she must have some fresh air, and decided to run away. So she ran out of Jane's mouth and right into Linda's.

At first Linda's please was annoyed because it didn't think there was enough room for two Pleases in one mouth. Jane's Please begged to be allowed to stay and when Linda's Please heard what it had to say, it took pity and allowed it to stay for the day. Linda's Please said: "When Linda uses me, we'll both go out together. She is kind, and I'm certain she would not mind saying 'Please' twice."

At lunch-time, Linda wanted some water and she asked, "Dad, will you pass me the water, please - please."

Everyone, including Linda herself, was puzzled by the second Please. Shortly afterwards Linda wanted some more potatoes, so she said, "Mum, pass the potatoes please - please."

Her mother laughed and as she passed the potatoes she asked, "Why do you say 'please' twice?"

"I don't know," answered Linda. "The words just seem to jump out for no reason. Jane, please - please, some more water."

Her father said, "Don't worry pet. You can never be too polite."

Jane was jealous that Linda was getting all her parents' attention so she decided she would see what happened if she said please - please. She asked, "Mum, can I have more potatoes p-p-p?"

She was trying very hard to say Please even once but how could she when her own Please was in Linda's mouth? So she tried again, and asked for some peas: "Dad will you give me more peas p-p-p?"

That was all she could say. This went on all day with Linda saying "Please. Please" all the time and Jane trying and failing to say Please. By night-time everyone in the house was getting tired of the whole thing.

As agreed, Jane's Please left Linda's mouth at midnight. Jane's Please never felt so well because it was used so much during the day.

The next morning at breakfast it got a huge suprise when Jane said, "Dad, will you get me some orange juice please." Jane was thrilled. The word had come out as easily as could be. It sounded every bit as good as when Linda said it and Linda was only saying one 'please' that morning. And from that day on, Jane was every bit as polite as her sister.

Don't Give Up (Traditional)

A little steam engine had a long train of cars to pull.

She went along great until she came to a steep hill. But then, no matter how much she tried, she just couldn't move the long train of cars. She pulled and pulled. She puffed and puffed. She backed and tried again. Choo! Choo! Choo! Choo!

Alas, all to no avail. The cars just couldn't get up the hill.

At last she left the train and started up the track alone. She wasn't giving up. She was seeking help. Over the hill and up the track went the little steam engine. Choo, choo! Choo, choo! Choo, choo!

Soon she saw a big steam engine standing on a side-track. He looked huge and strong. When she asked him for help, the big steam engine laughed, "Don't you see that I am through with my day's work? I have to get ready for tomorrow. I've no time to be helping the likes of you."

The little steam engine was disappointed, but on she went. Choo, choo! Choo, choo! Choo, choo!

Soon she came to a second huge steam engine on a side-track. He was huffing and puffing, as if he was exhausted.

"He may help me," thought the little steam engine. She ran up to him and said, "Will you help me bring my train of cars over the hill? It's too heavy for me."

The second big steam engine said, "You stupid, tiny train. Don't you see I'm exhausted? Can't you get some other engine to help you?"

Again the little steam engine was sorry but she kept going. Choo, choo! Choo, choo! Choo, choo!

Much later she came to another little steam engine. She rang alongside and said, "Will you help me over the hill with my train of cars? It's too heavy for me."

"Yes, indeed!" said the second little steam engine. "I'll be glad if I can."

So the little steam engines started back to where the train of cars had been standing all this time. One little steam engine went to the head of the train, and the other to the end of it.

Puff, puff! Chug, chug! Choo, choo!

Gradually the cars began to move. Gradually they climbed the steep hill. As they climbed, each little steam engine began to sing.

"I-think-I-can! I-think-I-can! I-think-I-can! I think-I-can! I-think-I-can . . ."

And they did! Soon, they were over the hill and going down the other side. Soon they were on the plain again, and the little steam engine could pull her train herself. So she thanked the little engine who had come to help her, and said goodbye.

And as she went merrily on her way, she sang to herself,

'I-thought-I-could!   I-thought-I-could!   I-thought-I-could! I-thought-I-could! I-thought-I-could!'

Count that Day Lost

If you sit down at set of sun
And count the acts that you have done,
And, counting, find
One self-denying deed, one word
That eased the heart of him who heard,
One glance most kind
That fell like sunshine where it went -
Then you may count that day well spent.

But if, through all the livelong day,
You've cheered no heart, by yea or nay -
If, through it all
You've nothing done that you can trace
That brought the sunshine to one face -
No act most small
That helped some soul and nothing cost-
Then count that day as worse than lost.

– George Eliot

A Father's Love

During the Vietnam war an American soldier wrote a letter to his son, in which he seeks to give good advice about how to live a good life. The soldier died in action and the letter remained unfinished.

My dearest Phil,

In the last few months everything has become very clear to me. I have discovered the difference between the important and the trivial. Here is what I ask of you:
Worry about courage
Worry about goodness
Worry about family
Worry about friendship
Worry about honour
Worry about getting a good education
Worry about living a good life
Worry about making a difference
Worry about understanding people
Above all worry that you are making the best of your life
and if you are bringing pain to another.
Don't worry about popular opinion
Don't worry about setbacks
Don't worry about the past
Don't worry about the future
Don't worry about growing up

Don't worry about anybody getting ahead of you
Don't worry about triumph
Don't worry about failure unless it comes through
your own fault . . .

Dead Certain

I was picking through the frozen turkeys at the local supermarket but I couldn't find one big enough for the family. I asked a passing assistant, "Do these turkeys get any bigger?"

The assistant replied, "I'm afraid not, they're dead."

The Blind Leading the Blind

Eamon deValera attended every All-Ireland final during his presidency - even though by the end of his reign he was almost totally blind. One of his later All-Irelands had a number of controversial refereeing decisions. The losing manager was asked for his thoughts afterwards. He observed: "Dev saw more of the game than the ref did."

Wise man's bluff

Sometimes it pays to bluff. Big John rode into town, tied up his horse and walked into the saloon.

"Give me a shot of red eye," said John.

He downed it in one and then walked outside. He noticed that his horse was gone so he came back inside the saloon. "If my horse isn't returned after I've had another drink," said John, "the same thing will happen here that happened in Dodge City. Now, give me another red eye."

He downed the red eye in one and walked outside to find his horse tied up against the rail. He mounted up and was just about to ride off when a cowboy walked up to him.

"Say, John," said the cowboy. "What happened in Dodge City?"

"I had to walk home," John replied.

Give a Little Respect

My mother always had some reservations about my decision to become a teacher. She rightly pointed out that at the time teachers were very well-respected but earned very little money. She used to say that I would be better if I had a job with a little less respect and a little more money!

Genius

....

Once there was a thirsty seagull. She had flown inland during the summer and was badly in need of a drink. At last she saw a bowl outside some stables. She flew down and saw that it held a tiny amount of water, but it was so low in the bowl that she could not reach it.

"But I must have some water," she cried. "I'm too tired to fly any farther. What shall I do? I know! I'll knock the basin over."

She beat it with her wings, but it was too heavy. She could not move it.

Then she thought for a few minutes. "I've got it. I'll break it. Then I'll drink the water as it pours out. How good it will taste."

With beak and claws and wings she threw herself against the basin. But it was too strong.

The poor seagull paused for breath. "There must be a way, if only I had the wit to find it out."

After a short break, the seagull had a brainwave. There were many small stones lying about. She picked them up one by one and dropped them into the basin. Slowly the water rose, until finally she could drink it.

The seagull said to herself, "There is always a way out of hard places if only you have the wit to find it."

Tall tales

I like the story of the man on his death bed who has five sons, four are giants but tiny Tim is a scrawny little fella. With almost his last breath John asked his wife Mary: "Is tiny Tim really mine?"

Mary replied straight from the heart: "Oh, John he is. I swear to God."

With that a smile crossed John's face and he died peacefully. Mary whispered a soft prayer: "Thanks be to you God for not letting him ask about the other four."

Threesome

The Chinese understanding of happiness is interesting. They analysed happiness and they decided that it was broken into three elements. The first was to have something in life to work for. The second was to have something in life to dream for. The third was to have someone to love. Some have luck in each of these three fronts, but they have to work at it.

Empowerment

Go with the people
Live with them
Learn from them
Love them
Start with what they know
Build with what they have
But with the best leaders
When the work is done
The task accomplished
The people will say
'We have done this ourselves'.

– Lao Tsu, China

Listen and Learn

Bobby: "Dad, are caterpillars good to eat?"

Dad: "Don't talk about such things at the dinner table. We'll discuss it later."

Bobby after dinner: "Never mind, Dad. That caterpillar was on your salad, but he's all gone now."

Forward Planning

Little Susan had forgotten her best friend's birthday and sat down to write a letter of apology. It read as follows: "Dear Julia. I beg your forgiveness for forgetting your birthday and it would serve me right if you forgot my birthday next Friday."

Right and Wrong

It takes a big person to admit when they are wrong but an even bigger one to keep their mouth shut when they are right.

Musical Chairs

A famous politician was once asked how he arranged the seating of the notables who attended his dinner parties. He replied: "I don't bother about who sits where. Those who matter don't mind and those who mind don't matter."

The Absent-Minded Professor

An absent-minded professor was approached by a gushing female at a dinner-party. "Don't you remember me, Professor?" she asked.

"I'm afraid not."

"Well, many years ago you asked me to marry you." she said.

"Really? And did you?"

The Odd Couple

An American tourist and his wife were visiting a cemetery. They were a bit surprised at one inscription they read on an old tombstone which said: "Here lies a politician and an honest man."

The wife said: "Fancy burying those two in the same grave!"

Don't Jump to Conclusions

The manager was listening to his clerk on the phone in the department store who was saying: "I love you dear. Only you. Devoted to you. These miss-you-nights are the longest. I will always love you. You to me are everything."

The manager became irate and snapped at her icily when she put down the phone: "Miss Hall, that telephone has been fixed where it is for the purpose of transacting business and not for love-making during business hours. Don't let it occur again."

Miss Hall: "I was just ordering some new songs for Department Five, sir."

Rough Justice

....

A farmer and a butcher were engaged in a law suit against each other over a plot of land. The case was listed for the Christmas session. The lawyer engaged by the farmer said to his client: "I'm afraid we have no hope of winning the case."

The farmer asked: "Supposing as it's Christmas time, I sent a nice turkey with my name on it to the judge, would that help?"

"That would ruin our chances completely," said the lawyer.

When the case was heard the judge found in favour of the farmer. "I can't understand how we won," said the lawyer.

"It must be the turkey I sent to him."

"You did?!", gasped the lawyer.

The farmer answered: "I did, but I put the other fellow's name on it."

All Creatures Great and Small

The great Irish poet William Butler Yeats was going home from work one cold winter's evening. Having failed to find a coat hanger that morning, he had casually thrown his overcoat at the foot of the Abbey Stage. However, when he went back for it that evening, a little kitten had snuggled up inside the coat and was now fast asleep. Rather than disturb the kitten it is said that Yeats went backstage, got a pair of scissors, cut the section of his coat that was sheltering the kitten and headed out into the cold night air with a big hole in his coat.

You're So Vain

A spiteful seagull once collected a piece of meat. She flew to her nest and held the meat in her beak - savouring the moment. A fox, watching in the grass, coveted the piece of meat, so he shouted up at the bird: "How beautiful you are, you sweet creature. Your feathers are fairer than any bird I have ever seen. If your voice is even half as sweet, you must be without doubt the queen of all the birds in the forest."

Vanity got the better of the bird so she started to sing, but she dropped the meat. The fox grabbed the piece of meat and ran away.

Little Things Mean a Lot

Once there was a great king who was preparing to go to war and sent his servant to the blacksmith to be certain his horse was ready. The blacksmith told the groom he had no iron to shoe the horse, so the king would have to wait. The groom said this was not on and he would make do with what he had. The blacksmith tried his best, but he did not have enough iron nails to correctly fasten the fourth shoe.

The battle began in earnest. The king was leading his troops from the front when his horse's shoe fell off. The horse stumbled and rolled over. The king was thrown to the ground. His men deserted him when they saw his plight. The king was captured and the battle was lost. And all because of a missing nail.

All Creatures Meek and Tall

A man was passing through the West of Ireland and stopped to ask a farmer for the time. "Just a moment," said the farmer. He crouched down beside a cow in the pasture and lifted the udder very gently. "Ten past three," was the reply.

The man was astounded, "How can you tell time just by feeling a cow's udder?"

"Come here and I'll show you," said the farmer. "If you crouch down like this and lift up the udder, you can just see the church clock up the hill there."

A Bonnie Baby

My uncle Jack can be a little forgetful. Shortly after he became a grandfather some relatives came to visit when he was babysitting.

"May we see the new baby?" one asked.

"Not yet," said Jack. "I'll make coffee and we can chat first."

Thirty minutes had passed, and other relative asked, "May we see the baby now?"

"No, not yet," replied Jack.

After another half an hour had elapsed, they asked again, "May we see the baby now?"

"No, not yet," replied Jack.

Growing very impatient, they asked, "Well, when can we see the baby?"

"When it cries."

"When it cries? Why do we have to wait until it cries?"

"Because I forgot where I put it."

Self-help

G. K. Chesterton was once asked what book he would most likely to take with him if he was forced to live on a desert island. Chesterton replied: "First and foremost an instruction book on how to build a boat!"

The Creation of the Teacher

The Good Lord was creating teachers. It was His sixth day of 'overtime' and He knew that this was a tremendous responsibility, for teachers would touch the lives of so many impressionable young children. An angel appeared to Him and said, "You are taking a long time to figure this one out."

"Yes," said the Lord, "but have you read the specs on this order?"

TEACHER:

...must stand above all students, yet be on their level

...must be able to do 180 things not connected with the subject being taught

...must run on coffee and leftovers

...must communicate vital knowledge to all students daily and be right most of the time

...must have more time for others than for herself/himself

...must have a smile that can endure through pay cuts, problematic children, and worried parents

...must go on teaching when parents question every move and others are not supportive

... must have six pairs of hands.

"Six pairs of hands," said the angel, "that's impossible."
"Well," said the Lord, "it is not the hands that are the problem. It is the three pairs of eyes that are presenting the most difficulty!"

The angel looked incredulous, "Three pairs of eyes . . . on a standard model?"

The Lord nodded His head. "One pair can see a student for what he/she is and not what others have labelled him as. Another pair of eyes is in the back of the teacher's head to see what should not be seen, but what must be known. The eyes in the front are only to look at the child as he/she 'acts out' in order to reflect, 'I understand and I still believe in you', without so much as saying a word to the child."

"Lord," said the angel, "this is a very large project and I think you should work on it tomorrow."

"I can't," said the Lord, "for I have come very close to creating something much like Myself. I have one that comes to work when he/she is sick.....teaches a class of children that do not want to learn....has a special place in his/her heart for children who are not his/her own..... understands the struggles of those who have difficulty.... never takes the students for granted..."

The angel looked closely at the model the Lord was creating. "It is too soft-hearted," said the angel.

"Yes," said the Lord, "but also tough. You can not imagine what this teacher can endure or do, if necessary."

"Can this teacher think?" asked the angel.

"Not only think," said the Lord, "but reason and compromise."

The angel came closer to have a better look at the model and ran his finger over the teacher's cheek.

"Well, Lord," said the angel, "your job looks fine but there is a leak. I told you that you were putting too much into this model. You can not imagine the stress that will be placed upon the teacher."

The Lord moved in closer and lifted the drop of moisture from the teacher's cheek. It shone and glistened in the light.

"It is not a leak," He said, "It is a tear."

"A tear? What is that?" asked the angel. "What is a tear for?"

The Lord replied with great thought, "It is for the joy and pride of seeing a child accomplish even the smallest task. It is for the loneliness of children who have a hard time fitting in and it is for compassion for the feelings of their parents. It comes from the pain of not being able to reach some children and the disappointment those children feel in themselves. It comes often when a teacher has been with a class for a year and must say good-bye to those students and get ready to welcome a new class."

"My," said the angel, "The tear thing is a great idea... You are a genius!!" The Lord looked sombre. "I didn't put it there."

– Author Unknown

Father, Dear Father

God took the strength of a mountain,
The majesty of a tree,
The warmth of a summer sun,
The calm of a quiet sea,
The generous soul of nature,
The comforting arm of night,
The wisdom of ages,
The power of the eagles' flight,
The joy of a spring morning,
The faith of a mustard seed,
And the depth of a family need.
Then God combined these qualities
And there was nothing more to add.
He knew his masterpiece was complete
And so he called it DAD.

– Author Unknown

The Last Time

....

From the moment you hold your baby in your arms,
you will never be the same.
You might long for the person you were before,
When you have freedom and time,
And nothing in particular to worry about.
You will know tiredness like you never knew it before,
And days will run into days that are exactly the same,
Full of feedings and burping,
Nappy changes and crying,
Whining and fighting,
Naps or a lack of naps,
It might seem like a never-ending cycle.
But don't forget ...
There is a last time for everything.
There will come a time when you will feed
your baby for the very last time.
They will fall asleep on you after a long day
And it will be the last time you ever hold your sleeping child.
One day you will carry them on your hip then set them down,
And never pick them up that way again.
You will scrub their hair in the bath one night
And from that day on they will want to bathe alone.
They will hold your hand to cross the road,
Then never reach for it again.
They will creep into your room at midnight for cuddles,
And it will be the last night you ever wake to this.
One afternoon you will sing 'The Wheels on the Bus'

and do all the actions,
Then never sing them that song again.
They will kiss you goodbye at the school gate,
The next day they will ask to walk to the gate alone.
You will read a final bedtime story and wipe your last
dirty face.
They will run to you with arms raised for the very last time.
The thing is, you won't even know it's the last time
Until there are no more times.
And even then, it will take you a while to realise.
So while you are living in these times,
remember there are only so many of them
and when they are gone, you will yearn for just one more
day of them.
For one last time.

– Author Unknown

Mrs President?

....

While walking down the street one day a female head of state is tragically hit by a car and dies. Her soul arrives in Heaven and is met by St Peter at the entrance.

"Welcome to Heaven," said St Peter. "Before you settle in, it seems there is a problem. We seldom see a high official around these parts, you see, so we're not sure what to do with you."

"No problem, just let me in," says the lady.

"Well, I'd like to but I have orders from higher up. What'll we do is have you spend one day in Hell and one in Heaven. Then you can choose where to spend eternity."

"Really, I've made up in my mind. I want to be in Heaven," says the head of state.

"I'm sorry, but we have our rules." And with that, St Peter escorts her to the elevator and she goes down, down, down to Hell. The doors open and she finds herself in the middle of a golf course. In the distance is a club and standing in front of it are all her friends and the politicians who worked with her. Everyone is very happy and in evening dress. They greet her, hug her, and reminisce about the good times they had while getting rich at the expense of the people. They play a friendly game of golf and then dine on lobster. Also present is the Devil, who really is a very friendly guy and has a good time dancing and telling jokes. They are having such a good time that, before she realises it, it is time to go. Everyone gives her a big hug and waves while the elevator rises. The elevator goes up, up, up and reopens on Heaven, where St Peter is waiting for her.

"Now it's time to visit Heaven." So 24 hours pass with the head of state joining a large number of contented souls moving from cloud to cloud, playing the harp and singing. Before she realises it, the 24 hours have gone by and St Peter returns. "Well then, you've spent a day in Hell and another in Heaven. Now choose your eternal destination."

She reflects for a minute, then the head of state answers, "Well, I would never have expected it. I mean Heaven has been delightful, but I think I would be better off in Hell."

So St Peter escorts her to the elevator and she goes down, down, down to Hell. The doors of the elevator open and she is in the middle of a barren land covered with garbage. She sees all her friends, dressed in rags, picking up the trash and putting it in bags. The Devil comes over to her and lays his arm on her neck.

"I don't understand," stammers the head of state, "Yesterday I was here and everyone was on the golf course and we ate lobster and caviar and danced and had a great time. Now it is a wasteland full of garbage and my friends look miserable."

The Devil looks at her, smiles and says, "Yesterday we were campaigning. Today you voted for us!"

Ocean Deep

....

This story is about a little wave, bobbing along, having great fun. Everything is great until he notices the other waves in front of him, crashing against the shore. He is disconsolate when he realises that this is going to be his fate. Another wave comes by and notices how bad he is looking and asks, "Why do you look so sad?" The first wave says, "You don't understand! We're all going to crash. All of us waves are going to be nothing. This is tragic."

The second wave says, "No. You don't understand. You're not a wave. You're part of the ocean."

Love and Marriage

....

Marriage is like a bicycle made for two: when at different times one partner has to pedal harder than the other.

The Last Word

....

A woman was having her 104th birthday. The intrepid reporter from the local newspaper came and asked, "What's the best thing about being 104?"

The woman paused theatrically before replying in a strong voice, "No peer pressure!"

3

Close Encounters of the Personal Kind

Sometimes we meet people who have no airs but have amazing graces. In my life I have been lucky enough to meet some extraordinary people with exceptional insights into life and living. In this chapter I remember some of them. I also include some other real-life true stories.

The People's Saint: Mother Teresa

In her remarkable life Mother Teresa left an enduring imprint on the conscience and consciousness of the world because of her compassion and her work for the poor. This tiny Albanian nun, winner of the Nobel Peace Prize, with her hands joined in the Indian gesture of greeting, taught the world the meaning of compassion. She believed in St Augustine's idea of "mingling mercy with misery". She was the 'people's saint'.

Mother Teresa did not simply preach compassion - she lived it. She made personal, intimate contact in her daily life with the rejected, the homeless, the sick, the dying, the old, the lonely and prisoners. Not only did she devote her life to marginalised people, but she inspired others to follow her and, most importantly, by her love and attention to them, she rendered the invisible people of the world visible and she brought the most brutalised, rejected and marginalised people of the world to the centre of the stage. She showed us not only that those rejected by society need our love and our help, but that they have a vital role to play in calling the world to justice.

Perhaps the heart of Mother Teresa's understanding was the realisation that her work was not an achievement but simply something done for its own sake, something beautiful for God. She reminds us that there's nothing as important as the eternal. The life and passion of a person leaves an imprint on the ether of a place. Mother Teresa left quite an imprint.

We need people to fire our imaginative lives with the vision of life's possibilities. Mother Teresa showed us the way of passionate intensity. Perhaps the greatest thing she continues to do is to inspire people to do good things. Mother Teresa shows us how to make the right choices and to have a heart that never hardens, a temper that never tires, a touch that never hurts.

In 1992 I wrote to Mother Teresa, more in hope than in confidence, seeking an interview with her. To my astonishment she wrote to me and invited me to meet her when she came to Dublin to receive the Freedom of the City Award the following year.

The Emerald Isle

Many elements of her story are familiar, such as winning the Nobel Prize for Peace in 1979, but what is often forgotten is her deep affinity with Ireland. The order she chose to join was an Irish one, the Loreto Sisters, and she began her time as a nun by serving two months as a novice in Rathfarnham in 1928. Her ties with Ireland remained strong. She returned many times, was awarded the Freedom of the City of Dublin in 1993, and at the height of the Troubles in 1971 sent a group of her sisters to Belfast armed with just bedrolls and a violin to help "in whatever little way" they could. Even after her death, her Irish connections remain as her sisters continue to work in each of the four provinces: Dublin, Blarney, Sligo and Armagh.

When she initially applied to the Loreto order in Bengal she was told that she must first go to the Loreto Abbey in Rathfarnham, Dublin, where she needed to learn English, before she could journey to India. On 26 September 1928 she left for Dublin by train. It was the last time she ever saw her mother.

My final question to Mother Teresa was if Ireland held a unique place in her affections. With a shy smile and almost a whisper she answered:

"By blood and origin I am all Albanian. My citizenship is Indian. I am a Catholic nun. As to my calling, I belong to the whole world – and to Jesus. The people of the world are my people, but I will always have a special place in my heart for Ireland."

Blessed are the Peacemakers

Over the years the theme of Mother Teresa which returns to me like a refrain is her desire for peace. The job of a saint is to inspire us to be the best we can be. Now that she is a saint, she speaks to our troubled times in a quiet but powerful way, to call us to peace.

In an interview Mother Teresa was once asked if the taking of life was ever justified, in war, for example. She replied simply by shaking her head. The interviewer probed further and reminded her that the Church teaches us that there can be a just war. Mother Teresa continued to shake her head and said: "I can't understand it." The journalist was still not placated and asked: "Catholics have to believe that teaching?"

Mother Teresa instantly replied: "Then I am not a Catholic."

I reminded her that in 1981, when, after she returned from a mission to Ethiopia where a terrible drought threatened thousands of lives, she had written to President

Ronald Regan. The American president telephoned her on behalf of the American people and promised her that he would rush in the food and medicine she requested. Did she ever think about using that kind of power more often?

"I won't mix in politics. War is the fruit of politics, and so I don't involve myself, that's all. If I get stuck in politics, I will stop loving. Because I will have to stand by one not by all. This is the difference."

Accordingly, she advocated a spiritual solution:

"A beautiful thing happened in Calcutta. Two young people came to see me, Hindu people. They gave me a very big amount of money. 'How did you get so much money?' I asked them. They answered me, 'We got married two days ago. Before our marriage, we decided we would not have a big wedding feast and we would not buy wedding clothes. We decided that we would give the money we saved to you to feed the people.' In a rich Hindu family, it is a scandal not to have special wedding clothes and not to have a wedding feast. 'Why did you do that?' I asked them. They answered me, 'Mother, we love each other so much that we wanted to obtain a special blessing from God by making a sacrifice. We wanted to give each other this special gift.' Is that not beautiful? Things like that are happening every day, really beautiful things. We must pull them out. We have to pull out the wonderful things that are happening as well as the bad things.

"A Hindu man was once asked: 'What is a Christian?' He responded, 'The Christian is someone who gives.'" Give until it hurts, until you feel the pain.

"When I visited China in 1969, one of the Communist party asked me: 'Mother Teresa what is a communist to you?' I answered, 'A child of God, a brother, a sister of mine.' 'Well, you think highly of us. But where did you get that idea?' I told him, 'From God himself. He said, truly I tell you, just as you did it to one of the least of these who are members of my family, you did it to me.'"

Walk the talk

For Mother Teresa, talk was cheap:

"We all need to be generous. Once we had a great short-age of sugar in Calcutta. One day, a boy about four years old came to see me with his parents. They brought me a small container of sugar. When they handed it to me, the little one told me: 'I have spent three days without eating any sugar. Take it. This is for your children'. Although he could hardly say my name the little one loved with an intense love. We all need to learn from him."

The power of love

Love was central to Mother Teresa's vision:

"I was once walking down the street and a beggar came to me and said: 'Mother Teresa, everybody's giving to you, I also want to give to you. Today I got just a few small coins and I want to give them to you.' I thought for a second because if I took it he would have nothing to eat tonight, but if I don't take it I will hurt his feelings. So I put out my hands and I took the money. I have never seen such joy on anybody's face as I saw on his, that a beggar, he too, could give to Mother Teresa. It was a big sacrifice for him because it was all he had. It was beautiful. It was such a tiny amount that I could do nothing with it, but as he gave it up and I took it, it became like a fortune because it was given with so much love. So my message to the people of Ireland is love until it hurts."

A Smile for God: Desmond Tutu

The late Pope John Paul I was known as the 'smiling Pope'. Desmond Tutu is the laughing archbishop – a man who wears his humanity on his sleeve. When I was a boy, one of my favourite songs was 'What A Beautiful Noise' by Neil Diamond. To anyone lucky enough to meet him, the beautiful noise will always be the sound of Desmond Tutu's great heartfelt laugh – a sound resonant with warmth, sincerity and humanity. It is a shock to find how relaxed the former Nobel Peace Prize winner is – even though as one of the best-known faces in the world he is constantly in demand.

Although Desmond Tutu is clearly shaped by his life in South Africa, he has a wide number of contacts with Ireland. The Troubles in Northern Ireland and the efforts to find reconciliation afterwards mirrors the struggle in his country to find peace after the bitter divisions of the apartheid regime.

"For far too long we in South Africa, as in the North of Ireland, have been defined in terms of what we are against. Surely the time has come for us to be defined more by what we are for. This raises two crucial questions: What values do we witness to? How do we give witness?

"In this perspective the Church does not in any way diminish its vocation to confess and preach Christ when it recognises that the mystery of his salvation offers an embrace of healing mercy in which everyone has a place. On the contrary, it acknowledges that in the many paths that people follow in search of happiness and good, there is a common aspiration, written in hearts and in consciences by the Creator of the world, which is the aspiration for peace. My vision is for a dialogue between the religious traditions where each should without giving up their difference seek to realise their shared hope. They should stand shoulder-to-shoulder with one another and commit themselves to justice and peace for the good of all. Thus they can be a blessing to one another and the world."

I discovered upon meeting him that Archbishop Tutu has a surprisingly in-depth knowledge of Irish history. A particular area of fascination for him is the Irish famine.

"The Ireland of the 1840s was a vision of hell - the years of a tragedy beyond belief when over a million people on this tiny island died from famine. Nothing prepared people for it. Nothing could prepare anyone for the sight and smell of death on a massive scale - bundles of corpses where once there had been life.

I think this is a major reason why so many Irish people have worked to help the poor in the developing world as either missionaries or aid workers. I think because of their own experience of famine the Irish people have such an obvious sympathy for the needy and the poor in the developing world. I think Irish Christians feel the need to be in solidarity with the poor because they have such devotion to the Eucharist. Sharing the bread and wine symbolises the bond of love which unites us all in God's spirit and in that way creates an authentic community."

Desmond Tutu admires many people. One of his heroines is a little surprising:

"I have a great devotion to Thérèse of Lisieux. In her whole life she fought for a 'higher way', a deeper intimacy with God and a faith that challenged others to put God first. As I am not part of the Catholic tradition I think my interest in her indicates that she has an ecumenical appeal.

"At the centre of her spirituality is prayer. C.S. Lewis is back in vogue now following the cinematic treatment of his *Chronicles of Narnia*. In his play *Shadowlands* Lewis wrote: 'That's not why I pray, Harry. I pray because I can't help myself. I pray because I'm helpless. I pray because the need flows out of me all the time, waking and sleeping. It doesn't change God, it changes me.'

"I think that is part of Thérèse's appeal to us today. She encourages us to grasp the significance of retracting into oneself for inner peace, to seek solitude, silence and waiting, to be with God. It can't have been easy to reach such a prominent position in the Church at a time when women were often seen rather than heard."

Live Nun Running: Sr Helen Prejean

The enduring memory of a meeting with Sr Helen Prejean is that she smiles a lot. Yet her work campaigning against the death penalty is not conducive to laughter. Her gripping autobiographical book *Dead Man Walking* was nominated for the Pulitzer Prize and also won the 1994 American Library Association Notable Book of the Year. The acclaimed film director Tim Robbins was so inspired by Helen's book that he adapted it for the screenplay of his movie of the same name which starred Susan Sarandon in an Oscar winning role. The 1995 film has brought Helen and her work to millions around the world.

Over twenty years ago I watched that film in the Adelphi Cinema in Dublin. I remember the day as if it was yesterday. Such was the emotional intensity that the packed house streamed out in total silence to an uncharacteristically sunny O'Connell Street. In 1999 I heard she was coming to Dublin as part of her campaigning work against the death penalty and I wrote to her seeking an interview. Given the darkness of her ministry I was expecting somebody grave and terribly serious. Boy was I in for a surprise! She had a smile brighter than a lighthouse and a joy for life that was simply intoxicating.

In 1982 when she was invited to write to a prisoner on Death Row who brutally killed two teenagers, Sr Helen had little idea how much it would change her life. Although she abhorred his crime, she befriended the man, Patrick Sonnier, as he faced the electric chair.

"The previous year I had moved to work in a parish in New Orleans. At the time my main concern was not to get shot as death was rampant - from guns, disease and addiction. Myself and the five other nuns were practically the only whites in the town and poverty and crime were high. The reason for my coming was tied in to what was happening in the Catholic Church at the time, seeking to harness religious faith to social justice. Back in 1971, the worldwide synod of bishops had declared justice a 'constitutive' part of the preaching of the Gospel," she said.

"The mandate to practice social injustice is unsettling because taking on the struggles of the poor invariably means challenging the wealthy and those who serve their interests. In 1980 my religious community, the Sisters of St Joseph of Medaille, had made a commitment to 'stand on the side of the poor', and I had assented - but I have to confess only reluctantly."

The invitation from a member of the Prison Coalition was to write to Patrick Sonnier, who was on Death Row for the murders of David LeBlanc and Loretta Bourque after Ms Bourque had been raped. Sr Helen would later discover that the actual murders were committed by Patrick's brother Eddie. However, Patrick was guilty of collusion. Nonetheless, because of the rigidities of the American legal system she was unable to get the courts to recognise this fact, with the result that Eddie was allowed to live but Patrick wasn't.

"I had been very naive because I always thought our system of justice was pretty good. How wrong I was! I think a lot of people are aware of the irregularities of the judicial system since the OJ Simpson case. We have a saying that 'them without the capital get the punishment' in America because those with the capital are never really punished. It frightens me to think that many people who were on Death Row have come off because they were shown to be innocent after they were convicted for murder."

Given the horrific crimes Patrick Sonnier was convicted for, did Sr Helen have any moral qualms about getting involved with him?

"I could not accept that the state planned to kill Patrick in cold blood, but the thought of the young victims haunted me at first. The details of the depravity stunned me. A boy and girl, their young lives budding, were just blown away. In sorting out my feelings and beliefs, there was one piece of moral ground of which I was absolutely certain: if I were to be murdered I would not want my murderer executed. I would not want my death avenged, especially by a government which can't be trusted to control its own bureaucrats or collect taxes equitably or fill a pothole, much less decide which of its citizens to kill," Sr Helen said.

"As I corresponded with Pat I began to notice something about him. In each of his letters he expressed gratitude and appreciation for my care and made no demands. He never asked for me. He only said how glad he was to have somebody to communicate with because he was so lonely. The sheer weight of his loneliness, his abandonment, drew me. I abhorred the evil he had done. But I sensed something, some sheer and essential humanness, and that led me to investigate how I could meet him.

"In Matthew 25 Jesus gave us the test for the way to follow him. 'I was hungry and you fed me. I was thirsty and you gave me to drink. I was in prison and you visited me.' I had never believed though that passage was meant to apply to me - but all of a sudden it did."

The problem was that she was not visiting just an ordinary prison; she was going to Death Row - which was a very emotional experience.

"My stomach was in knots. I was there for a two hour visit and I was very apprehensive until I met Patrick. He was freshly shaven and his black hair was combed into a wave in the front. All of us have been thought to think of people on Death Row as monsters but this man didn't seem like a monster. He was very lonely because no one was visiting him. His mother had visited him once but she was never able to go back."

Sr Helen's emotional toll was much deeper when after all the legal options had been exhausted she accompanied Patrick to his death after knowing him for two and a half years.

"They strapped him in the electric chair. A metal cap was placed on his head and an electrode was screwed in at the top and connected to a wire that came from a box behind the chair. He grimaced. He could not speak anymore. A grayish cloth was placed over his head. Then there were three clanks as the switch was pulled with pauses in between. Nineteen hundred volts, then they let the body cool, then five hundred volts, another pause, then nineteen hundred volts. Then the doctor checked him to confirm he was dead."

If Helen has no misgivings about her involvement Patrick Sonnier, she does have one regret about an aspect of her early involvement in this ministry.

"The one thing I should have done is to have contacted the victims's families. I didn't think they would want to have anything to do with me because of my campaign to save Patrick, but then I met Lloyd LeBlanc who had lost his son because of the Sonniers. He told me that he would have been very grateful for my support because there was so much pressure on him to advocate the death penalty for Patrick. Many people thought that if he loved his son properly he must push for the death penalty for his murderer," she said.

"He went to Patrick's execution, not for revenge, but hoping for an apology. Before sitting in the electric chair he had said, 'Mr LeBlanc, I want to ask your forgiveness for what me and Eddie done,' and Lloyd LeBlanc had nodded his head, signifying a forgiveness he had already given. He says that when he arrived with the sherrif's deputies there in the canefield to identify his son – 'laying down there with his two little eyes sticking out like bullets' - he prayed the Our Father. And when he came to the words, 'Forgive us our trespasses as we forgive those who trespass against us,' he had continued, and he said, 'Whoever did this, I forgive them.'

"He told me later that although it was in the middle of the night after the execution he went straight to his parish priest and asked him to hear his confession and he said, 'Father, tonight I've been a witness to something dirty.'

"Since Patrick I have journeyed with four other people to their deaths on Death Row and I am very conscious now of the families of the people who they have killed as well as the families of the people executed because they too become victims."

As a relentless campaigner against the death penalty, Sr Helen is a frequent visitor to Ireland - on this occasion as a guest of Lifelines, the organisation which encourages people to become pen-pals of people on Death Row.

"I can't stress enough just how important letters to people on Death Row are. They have no one to visit them in many cases and feel utterly alone and rejected so just to know that someone from Ireland or anywhere is concerned enough about them to take the time and the trouble to write to them means an awful lot to their self-esteem. People are confined to small cells the size of a bathroom and are experiencing sensory deprivation and completely cut off so imagine the lift a letter gives them. These letters really are lifelines to people who have nothing else to look forward to."

Another campaign close to Sr Helen's heart is to a moratorium on the use of the death penalty. She feels that there is an alternative to the 'eye for an eye' mentality.

"The way of Jesus is forgiveness. Forgiveness is never going to be easy. Each day it must be prayed for and struggled for and won."

A Man for All Seasons:
Gordon Wilson

....

'Where were you the night John F. Kennedy was shot?' This was a question I had often heard posed as I was growing up, but I never really understood the power of a single event to remain frozen in the memory until Remembrance Sunday, 1987 in Enniskillen, Co. Fermanagh. Immediately after the carnage caused by an IRA bomb during a parade in the town, communal passions threatened to explode. But even the hardest heart could not but have been melted by Gordon Wilson's intensely moving account of how he lay bleeding under the rubble, clutching his daughter's hand and heard her fading voice saying: "Daddy, I love you very much." In this highly-charged atmosphere, Gordon's words of forgiveness in a BBC interview only hours later diffused an extremely volatile situation.

I met him in Enniskillen less than a year after the death of his much-loved daughter, Marie, a young nurse. He untangled from the sea of dogma a simple message that true religion is about love, not hate - about reaching out in handshake and not with clenched fists.

"When I spoke that day I was only speaking for myself. I never envisaged that my words would have the impact they did. If I had time to reflect I would have wanted to be more eloquent but I think people seemed to respond better to sincerity than eloquence. Maybe there is an important lesson for us there," he said.

In his reaction to his daughter's murder, Gordon alerted us to the fact that forgiving and excusing are not simply different, but polar opposites. If one was not really to blame, then there is nothing to forgive. To excuse somebody who can really produce good excuses is not Christian charity; it is only fairness. To be a Christian means to forgive the inexcusable, because God has forgiven the inexcusable in us.

Excuses by themselves have a minimal value, since by definition they are powerless in the face of the inexcusable and the unjustifiable. Only forgiveness can achieve this. It is only through forgiveness that we are set free.

Throughout our history the abuse of religion has brought nothing but division to our troubled country. When Gordon Wilson forgave the inexcusable, he showed that Christianity is a potentially healing and unifying force in our society. In his darkest hour, his words of forgiveness showed that the gentleness of Christianity is stronger than a terrorist's bomb.

"Every father thinks that their own daughter is sweeter than everyone else's. I suppose I was no different. I think though she was a very good person. I know that sounds very pious and that kind of language is not fashionable today. I didn't want to contaminate Marie's memory by using dirty talk. Nothing that I could say was going to bring Marie back. I couldn't bring myself to wish hate on the people who killed my daughter. Not everybody understood. I am sad to report that I lost friends because of what I said that day, but I did what I thought was right and I am prepared to accept the consequences," he said.

"To be honest I am still shocked about the fuss I created. All I tried to do was to do what Jesus asked. As he hung on the cross, what did he say? 'Father forgive them they know not what they do.' If you are a Christian you have to at least try and live your life as Jesus asked. I'm not saying that is always easy. In fact a lot of the time it is really hard."

The tyranny of the past can be broken; the sin of the past can be healed in the future - not by minimising the seriousness of the past, but by putting the past in the perspective of a different future. No one understood this better than Gordon Wilson. He was a man who dedicated his final years to breaking free from the tyranny of the past and trying to put it in the perspective of in the perspective of a better future for our troubled island.

The physical legacy of the day of the explosion was most evident in the awkward way he tried to light a cigarette during our meeting. The bomb blast left him with diminished use of one hand. He fought bravely to disguise his annoyance with his incapacity.

"When you think of my physical sufferings from the bomb I got away very light. I can cope with it easy enough - it is much more difficult to cope with Marie's loss," he said.

"Have no doubts I had many a dark day since Marie died, but whenever I was at my lowest God sent me something to get me through it. People think I was very strong. I wasn't. I simply surrendered to God."

My abiding memory of him though is of an incident the day we met. As we spoke above his draper's shop in Enniskillen his two young grandchildren burst in the door. His serious face broke into the most magnificent, warm smile and his eyes lit up when he saw them.

To many people this soft-spoken native of County Leitrim will always be remembered as a man who embodied the Christian virtue of forgiveness. I remember him though, as I remember my own grandfather, as a man who doted on his grandchildren.

"I believe that for the sake of our children and our grandchildren we can't stay trapped in the past. For too long we have been like prisoners in cells. We must break free and end the 'them and us' mentality. We've got to change our attitudes and our mindsets. People have to understand it is not about negotiating convictions but about walking a path together," he said.

The Bruised, the Battered and the Broken: Peter McVerry

Nelson Mandela, John F. Kennedy, Mother Teresa and Mikhail Gorbachev. Four remarkable people who have left a distinctive imprint on the history of the world. In an Irish context what unites this famous four is that each of them have received the highest honour the state can confer on anybody – the Freedom Of The City of Dublin. Only 78 people, the best of the best, from home and abroad have received this honour. It is a small indication of Peter McVerry's contribution to Irish life that he is one of those chosen few. His lifelong commitment to the least, the last and the lost means that he is a prophetic voice in Irish society today.

Peter McVerry is a Jesuit priest who has been working with young people experiencing homelessness for more than 40 years. In 1974, Fr McVerry moved to Summerhill in Dublin's north inner-city where he witnessed first hand the problems of homelessness and deprivation. In 1979, he opened a small hostel to provide accommodation for home-less boys between the ages of 12-16. Four years later in 1983, he officially founded the Arrupe Society, a charity to provide housing and support for young people experiencing home-lessness as a response to the growing problem in Dublin. He subsequently set up the Peter McVerry Trust to help those on the margins of Irish society. In April 2018 he won a People of the Year Award for his commitment to helping others.

He has a lesser known claim to fame. He was the first coach of Irish rugby legend Ollie Campbell in Belvedere College, Dublin. So how good a rugby coach was he? Let's just say when they write the history of Irish rugby Peter's name will not be mentioned! Not even in the footnotes!

To know Peter is to inhabit a complex emotional space. Every time I meet him I come away inspired – because of his unwavering commitment to those who inhabit the constituency of the rejected. And yet I also come away feeling uncomfortable not because of what he says but because of who he is – he is the most challenging person I know because he reminds us of uncomfortable truths.

He is a reminder that we speak when we do not speak.

We act when we do not act.

Peter's message to us is that if all we think of is number one, we are not going to add up to very much.

His two twin calls are to mercy and compassion:

"When young people tell me they don't believe in God, I ask them to tell me about the God they don't believe in. I usually end up telling them that I don't believe in that God - a censorious, judgemental God - either; the God I believe in is a God of mercy and compassion, who is tolerant of our weaknesses and forgiving of our offences," he told me.

"How we understand God determines how we understand what God wants, and therefore it influences our attitudes, priorities and behaviour. When I was growing up, the God that was presented to me by the Church was a God who was a judge. God was essentially a lawgiver, who had formulated many laws by which we were to live our lives, laws that were affirmed and interpreted by the Church.

This God would judge us by our observance of those laws. If we obey them, we will be rewarded with a place in heaven; if we disobey them, we may lose God's friendship forever. God's passion was our observance of those laws.

"Every Sunday, then, I went to Mass in order to observe the law of God, to do my duty. One Sunday, I decided I was not going to go to Mass that day, and I didn't. I felt a great weight had been lifted off my shoulders. I had been going to Mass to fulfil an obligation that had been imposed on me. From then on, I went to Mass every Sunday, not because I felt under an *obligation* to go, but because I actively *chose* to go. The constant focus on obeying laws, in order to win God's favour, was oppressive. I was on a fast track to becoming a righteous little Pharisee."

The adult Peter has a very different understanding of God.

"Working with homeless people has made me question this understanding of God. I got close to people whose lives were full of suffering, who had experienced tragic childhoods, the effects of which continued into adulthood. And society often seemed indifferent to their plight, or worse still, judged and condemned them.

"The God of the law also appeared irrelevant to their lives. The chief concern of homeless people, like that of refugees fleeing war-torn Syria or impoverished sub-Saharan Africa, is about getting through *this* life, not about getting into the next one," he said.

"The God that I now believe in is a God who cares about the suffering and pain of God's children, a God whose passion is compassion. That God was revealed in the life and death of Jesus. Jesus was the compassion of God to the dispossessed and powerless, he shared meals with those who were rejected by the society of his time, he cured the sick ("feeling sorry for him, Jesus touched him and said to him 'be cleansed'." Mk 2:41). Finally, Jesus gave up his own life, so that we might live.

"Pope Francis' emphasis on the God of Mercy (mercy, he defined, as 'opening one's heart to wretchedness') is leading us into a different understanding of our relationship with God and has profound implications for the way we live our lives - and our spiritual lives. A spirituality which focuses on what *I* want (getting to Heaven) and on what *I* must do to achieve my goal (obeying God's laws) is replaced by a spirituality which focuses on what *others* need and what I must do to help them achieve *their* goal.

"To grow into the image and likeness of the God of compassion, we have to become the compassion of God to others. The God of compassion is 'good news to the poor' but far more threatening to the lifestyle and securities of those of us who are not poor than the God whose passion is the observance of the law."

From Sight to Insight: Richard Moore

The wound that will never heal. To many people in Derry that is the memory of 30th January 1972. On that fateful day British paratroopers shot 26 anti-internment marchers on the streets of Derry, killing 14 and wounding many more. Those killed were: Gerard Donaghy (17); James Wray (22); Gerard McKinney (35); William McKinney (26); John Young (17); William Nash (19); Michael McDaid (20); Michael Kelly (17); Kevin McElhinney (17); Patrick Doherty (31); Jack Duddy (17); Hugh Gilmore (17) and Bernard McGuigan (41). Shortly after that day John Johnston died prematurely of a brain tumour. His family is convinced that the trauma of Bloody Sunday contributed significantly to his untimely death.

Bloody Sunday marked a milestone in the unfolding history of the North. Internment had been introduced the previous August by the increasingly desperate Unionist regime at Stormont.

Television images captured the shock, the disbelief, the distress which the crowd felt when the shooting started and their terrible sense of helplessness as the death toll increased. The Troubles produced many unforgettable moments. However, one of the defining images of the Troubles will always be that of the late Bishop Edward Daly on Bloody Sunday, waving a white bloodstained handkerchief, as he led a group of men carrying the limp body of a teenager away from the hail of bullets and ever-mounting bloodbath.

The day was one of the watershed moments in Anglo-Irish history. The anger of all Ireland was reflected in the torching of the British Embassy in Dublin. Such was the reaction to Bloody Sunday that within two months the Stormont parliament was dissolved and direct rule instituted. Westminster assumed full responsibility for all other functions of government in the Six Counties. Bishop Edward Daly subsequently said, "What really made Bloody Sunday so obscene was the fact that people afterwards at the highest level of British justice justified it."

As a boy I could not make sense of the Troubles. On both sides of the divide there seemed to be unbearable pain and horrific cruelty. Most times I winced when I heard about yet another casualty. Yet from time to time there were stories that emerged of extraordinary heroism and considerable courage and compassion. When I heard of one man's story as an adult I felt I had to make my first ever trip to Derry just to meet him and hear his story at first hand.

The passing years have done nothing to diminish the memory of that meeting. As a ten-year-old in Derry, Richard Moore's family were directly affected by Bloody Sunday. His uncle, Gerard McKinney, was going to the assistance of a wounded man when he saw a British soldier in the alleyway. He raised his arms and shouted, "Don't shoot! Don't shoot!" The autopsy report on McKinney, who was just 35-years-old, supported the eye-witness claims that he had his hands in the air when shot. He left behind seven young children. A week after he was buried, his wife, Ita, gave birth to their eighth child, a baby boy whom she named Gerard.

Quite unbelievably, William McKinney (26) ran to the aid of Gerard (no relation). As he bent over his namesake, he was shot dead in the back. Richard has very vivid memories of this momentous moment.

"I remember the silence that fell on Derry that day. It was something out of the ordinary. I was out playing with my friends and suddenly I noticed my uncle calling to the house and then more relatives. Then I saw my mother was crying and she told me that her brother, Gerard, had been shot. It was very hard on her but I don't think any of us will ever appreciate exactly how tough the whole thing was for his wife Ita," he said.

"The other thing I remember most about Bloody Sunday was the funerals. I don't think I'll ever forget coming into the church and looking up to see the 13 coffins laid out side by side. That is a sight I will take with me to my grave."

Four months later, on the 4th of May, the Troubles cast an even deeper shadow on Richard's young life.

"I was walking home from school one day at twenty past three in the afternoon and as I walked past a British Army look-out post I remember passing it and that's all I remember. I found out later that a soldier let off his gun and I was struck by a rubber bullet in the head from about ten feet. I got hit in the bridge of my nose. I lost one eye and the other was rendered useless. I was taken away and laid out on a table in the school and a teacher who knew me very well saw me and didn't recognise me because my face was so badly damaged. I remember being taken away and the siren of the ambulance. As I was being take away in the ambulance, my father was with me. He wouldn't let my mother see me because he didn't want her to see me in that condition," Richard said.

"I'm sure when my mother heard about Bloody Sunday and Gerard she thought that was probably the end of it from her family but four months later the Troubles landed right smack back in the middle of their living room again and I was blinded for life because of that bullet. My mother and father were good, God-fearing people. They went to Mass every day. They never talked about politics and all of a sudden they had to face this double tragedy. My parents prayed a lot and it must have been prayer that got us through it. It could have been nothing else. When I learned that I would never see again I cried that I would never see my Mammy and Daddy again."

Unlike many of his contemporaries, Richard did not give in to bitterness.

"I'm not bitter. I bear no ill will towards the soldier who shot me and in fact I met him and told him that. Bitterness is a destructive emotion and only hurts the person who is bitter," he said.

"Make no mistake I have paid a heavy price for what happened to me on that day in 1972. I am married now and I have two daughters. I was there for their births and I would have given anything to be able to see what they looked like. Likewise when they made their first Holy Communion. I was there for them but I would've loved to have been able to see them. Christmas morning as they open their Christmas presents I would love to be able to see the smiles on their faces. So all those pleasures have been denied to me. I have lost a lot but I can forgive that soldier."

In partnership with Concern International, Richard established and directs the ecumenical 'Children in Crossfire' organisation to build bridges between the two communities. Rather than remaining a prisoner of history, he is at the frontier of shaping a new future in Northern Ireland where the traditional enmities are redundant.

"No family has better reason to remember Bloody Sunday than mine. No one knows better the damage the Troubles have caused than me. I carry it with me every moment of my life in a very real way. If I can forgive why can't others do the same?"

A Moment of Grace:
Sr Pauline Fitzwalter

An accident of history threw me into the company of Sr Pauline Fitzwalter, who is known as 'Sydney's Mother Teresa'. At 75 years of age she was still a human dynamo though her hearing was not what it once was. To visit her home, using the term loosely, was an experience. It was like a cross between a railway station and a refuge for the bewildered. Yet despite the constant flow of callers, there was a magical atmosphere about her apparently idiosyncratic community. In this frugal household, love was all around.

Irish blood flows through her veins. She grew up in an Australian town called Donnybrook. Her mother was the daughter of Patrick Joseph Murphy, who came from Galway, and Catherine Sarsfield, who came from an island on Lough Corrib. Her childhood, though, was anything but blissful:

"My parents were separated when I was three. My mother was pregnant when they split up. She was a great provider but I don't think she fully understood the importance of displaying affection to us. My father was an alcoholic. I have known what it was like to live in a dysfunctional family and I think this has given me a greater empathy for the people I work with today," she said.

After she finished school she decided to become a teacher, or in Australian parlance a 'school mam'. Then a friend asked her would she present a programme on radio and she went on to concentrate on women's and children's items. Around this time she became engaged to be married. During her engagement she came to realise that although her boyfriend loved her totally she did not love him in the same way. She broke off the engagement and threw herself into her work with such ferocity that physically, mentally and emotionally she was on the point of collapse:

"I was 23 at the time. I started feeling terrible pain behind in my eyes. I got a panic attack and I knew my heart was at least murmuring if I was not having an actual heart attack. I saw my face in the sideboard and it had gone purple. I wasn't afraid of dying but there was this question inside me: 'What have I done for others?' I knew I hadn't done much to hurt them but also I know that I hadn't done much to help them.

"My mother called for the priest first and then the doctor. That was her way, the eternal values were more important. The priest's name was Bertie Bree from Dublin. He didn't anoint me because you had to be literally on the verge of death before you were anointed at the time. Then the doctor came. It was not the first time he had visited me. When I was three I had convulsions and the same doctor had visited me and said I wouldn't make it through the night. I pulled through both times," she told me.

"Looking back now I don't think of it as a break down but as a breakthrough. As I made my recovery that question inside me, 'What have I done for others?' kept coming back to me. I knew my life would have to take a different route."

After much soul-searching, Pauline decided she would follow the path of her younger sister Bernice and become a Good Samaritan sister. In 1948, when she was 25 years of age, she entered their novitiate in Sydney. After her spiritual formation was completed and her education was extended, she returned to teaching. She subsequently became a lecturer in the novitiate. The whole course of her life was changed forever by a chance meeting in 1965:

"I was asked to be one of four usherettes who were to be responsible for directing the guests to their places at a ceremony in our convent where 17 of our young sisters were taking the veil. As the ceremony started the Mother Superior asked me to wait outside the gate and direct any latecomers to their places - which meant that I would miss the proceedings. At the time I believed that blind obedience gave glory to God, I don't any more, and waited outside.

"After a while a man came to the gate and I said to him: 'Good morning. Which sister are you looking for?' He replied: 'No sister in particular but could you help me I'm looking for peace. The name of your convent is Mount St Benedict and the Benedictine motto is *pax*.' I knew immediately he was an educated man and then he went on to say: 'I've just escaped from a mental home.' He looked very rational and had a book of Gerard Manley Hopkins' poetry in his hand and asked me if I liked Hopkins. He met me as a friend and I liked him immediately because there was a gentleness about him. He told me his name was Francis Webb. I had read a poem in the newspaper two weeks previously by a man called Francis Webb which had made a deep impression on me and he was one of the biggest names in Australian poetry at the time. I asked him if he was a poet but he said he was just a versifier.

"We had a rule in our congregation at the time which stated that whenever we had a lengthy conversation with any one we had to bring God into it. Looking back it was a very artificial notion but I raised the God question with him. He said: 'Sister I have lost everything people consider important but I have retained the two most important things in life - my faith in Christ and in the Church.'

"He went on to tell me that he had no place to go and what he really wanted at that stage was to get a lift to a St Vincent de Paul hostel some miles away. I was struck by how such a talented man had such a modest wish. I resolved there and then I would get him a lift. I remembered there was a young priest who hadn't bothered to attend the ceremony and who was sitting in the shade. He had said to me: 'I'm sick of the sight of convent chapels.' He seemed to be the obvious choice to take Francis to the hostel so I brought the poet over to him. I was shocked at the priest's arrogance. He dismissively told Francis to thumb a lift with the lorry drivers. It was like a bucket of water had been thrown over my face because I had led Francis to believe he would get help but all he got was rejection.

"As I watched Francis walked down the drive I had an inner vision of Christ, that's all I can say. I knew for certain I was sending away Christ. Francis had asked for a crumb but it had been snatched away from him. I fought hard to control my temper. I had a lengthy conversation with the priest. I said to him that man was Francis Webb. He said: 'You mean the poet? He was no more Francis Webb than you are.' We then went on to talk about the needy and he said there were no needy people any more. He knew that I was unhappy with his treatment of Francis and provoked me into saying: 'I don't know about you Father but the Gospel is still relevant to my life.' I knew I had struck a blow below the belt and I repented for my sin afterwards.

"A short time afterwards I spoke about the incident in detail to the Mother Superior. She could see that I had been deeply affected by the whole episode and suggested that we try to contact Francis. We went through the phone book and eventually we tracked down one of his relatives. Then the full story of Francis emerged. His mother died when he was a young boy and his father couldn't cope with the shock and was unable to care for Francis and his three sisters. They were brought up by their grandparents but really had a life of emotional deprivation. The relative was able to tell me the name of the psychiatric institution Frank was staying in.

"I wrote to him and asked him to pardon me and the priest who had humiliated him. When he got that letter he wrote straight back to me. He told me that he was in a strait jacket at the time and to know that another person was thinking of him in that way was like a miracle for him. We began to correspond and gradually I began to see the need for a new apostolate to people who would be considered 'down and outs' and had no one to love them. I resolved to do something about it. Francis asked me to keep the first place in this new caring community for him. Sadly on 23 November 1973 Francis died before I had started anything. Our Lord then started to work harder on me and in 1977 I asked to be released from my congregation.

"I moved to the inner city of Sydney in 1977 and set up

a new community for those who had no one to love them. Initially I was living with just three men which was very unusual at the time. In the first year we established a network of three houses for all kinds of victims of abuse and neglect. Over the years our community houses have mushroomed around Sydney and we look after all kinds of people ranging from children of five years old to men and women of 80. Our primary objective is to give people a sense that they are worthwhile, cared for and most importantly that they are loved. In the face of each of these people I see Christ. They have given me new horizons of hope in my life."

President Dwight D. Eisenhower once said: "Every gun that is made, every warship launched, every rocket fired, signifies a theft from those who hunger and are not fed, those who are cold and have not clothes. The world in arms is not spending money alone. It's spending the sweat of its labourers, the genius of scientists and the hopes of its children."

The late Michael Paul Gallagher S.J. likened Christian faith to the first smile of an infant. "For weeks you smile and express your love . . . then one day your baby smiles back. He or she has entered into a different relationship, has responded to all you have given. It is a moment of recognition, of love. Our life of faith is exactly like that in its core simplicity. God loves us in Christ and one day we must realise it . . . there is a danger of reducing faith to morality or to the externals of religious belonging. If that happens religion becomes a matter of 'I thought' or 'I ought not'. Needless to say the commandments come alive and make best sense if God's love is received and recognised - like that first smile."

Sr Pauline smiles often and I think that is significant.

Blind Ambition: Michael Hingson

As a boy one of the most traumatic experiences in my life was when our dog Lassie died. Growing up on a farm I always have had a huge admiration for people who work with dogs. That is why one man's dramatic story had a huge impact on me and why I was determined to meet him when he came to visit Ireland.

The memory of September 11, 2001 still has the power to chill the blood. It will forever remain a template for humankind's experience of evil, a black symbol of humanity. Within minutes our television sets brought the shocking reality into our homes with disturbing immediacy. The television images ensured that the event belonged to everyone. The mourning too, like that for Princess Diana, was a communal experience. We united to grieve but in a safe and private place, even amid millions of other viewers, to grapple with the sadness that enveloped us.

Yet even in these darkest moments there were accounts of courage and heroism. One of the stories that really moved me that emerged in the wake of the slaughter was that of Michael Hingson. Michael was born prematurely with the result that his retinas did not develop properly and he was born blind. From the start, though, he embraced a can-do philosophy.

"I grew up in a family where my parents insisted that I had the same responsibilities as everybody else. I learned to ride a bike and I had a paper round, so I grew up thinking I could function if I wanted to do so. I understood that my life was going to be what I was going to make it. So I worked. I got a Masters Degree in Physics. I got married," he said.

Learning to turn his blindness, an apparent liability, into an asset, Michael had made big advances in his career by September 11.

"I was at the time the regional manager for Quantum Corporation and had a sales force under me in the World Trade Centre. They were out of the office for the day but I had six guests with me for training. I was about to begin a training session with a graphic presentation. People are always impressed when a blind person does a graphic presentation.

"I was prepared to start the training at 8.45 when the airplane hit the building, though at the time we didn't know what happened. We were on the 78th floor on the south side of the building. The airplane hit on the 96th floor of the building on the north side so we were sheltered in some way. We didn't even hear the plane come in. We just felt this jolt and heard this kind of muffled explosion and the building began to tip over because literally the plane was pushing against it. We moved over about 15 feet and then the building reverted to its normal position," he told me.

"I had moved over to the nearest doorway because I'd always been told that was the safest place to avoid flying glass and so on. When the building stopped moving I went back into my office. My guide dog, Roselle, who had been under my desk asleep had woken up and understandably wanted to see what all the fuss was about. I took her leash to be certain that we wouldn't be separated from each other. Almost immediately my friend, David, who had been looking out the window said, 'Mike, my God there's fire above us and we need to evacuate right now.'

"Roselle wasn't nervous. I wasn't nervous because I didn't smell smoke though I heard things falling outside the window, but I was anxious we didn't evacuate until we got our six guests out of the building. David got our guests out towards the stairs. I rang my wife to tell her something had happened at the World Trade Centre but we were getting out because I knew she'd be watching the television."

If proof were ever needed that a dog is a man's best friend, what happened next to Michael is the definitive testament.

"People need to understand that a guide dog and its owner form a team and both parties have to do their jobs properly if the team is to work. Roselle's job is to guide us safely. She is a kind of pilot. My job is to tell us where we go. I'm the navigator. We started down the stairs and got out.

"We knew it was pretty serious and coming down the stairs there were people who were panicking. We smelled jet fuel coming down the stairs but we had no idea what had happened. We assumed an airplane had hit the building but we had no clue that a second plane had hit the other building," Michael said.

"We got outside and heard that the second tower also was on fire. We assumed that the flames from the first tower had somehow reached over to the second one. We decided to aim for the parking lot where David's car was parked. We were only about 100 metres from the parking lot when the tower collapsed. At first we heard a rumble and suddenly the noise became deafening and people literally ran for their lives. That was all you could do. It was every man for himself. Before the tower fell I was starting to panic. I have a very clear memory of saying to myself, 'God how could you take us out of one building only to let us die at the foot of a second one'. Immediately though another voice in my head said, 'Don't worry about what you can can't control. Focus on running with Roselle and the rest will take care of itself.' I might have been able to get down the stairs on my own but I'd never have been able to get away from the falling tower without Roselle.

"I was in shock. Certainly when the first tower fell we were struck by the enormity of what had happened and then only after the second tower fell was I able to get my wife on the cell phone and Karen told me then exactly what had happened."

After the experience Michael decided to give his life to the promotion of the work of the guide dogs association. What advice would he give to the parents of children who are blind?

"There are certain things they should do. Make sure they learn braille and how to use talking computers. Don't make the assumption that because your child is blind he or she shouldn't have the same responsibilities and standards. Just because I can't do the job the same doesn't mean I can't do the job - apart from certain obvious exceptions like driving a truck. Don't tell me I can't do the job show me how to do it. Don't put limitations but find opportunities. Blindness isn't the problem. It's the prejudices and short-sightedness of sighted people that cause the problems."

Operation Shamrock

One of my closest friends is a German, Helmut Sunder-mann. It was he who introduced me to a story that I had never heard of. Since the controversy about Brexit began this story has often returned to me as a metaphor for the importance of building bridges, not walls.

On March 23, 1997 the German President, Dr Roman Herzog, visited Ireland as a thank you to the country for giving safety and shelter to German refugees after the Second World War. Until very recently 'Operation Shamrock' was a forgotten chapter of Irish and European history.

In 1945 over 300 people attended the founding meeting of the Save the German Children Society in the Shelbourne Hotel. The motivations of these people were mixed. Dr Kathleen Murphy, a paediatrician, was appointed chairwoman. She claimed that they were concentrating on German people as they were the most "necessitous" and that as Christians they were obliged to assist "starving German children". Words from scripture were judiciously quoted:

"For I was a stranger and you gave me welcome, I was naked and you gave me clothes, I was hungry and thirsty and you gave me food and drink, I was in pain and you gave me comfort." (Matthew 25)

However, others had a very different motive. An army officer confessed that he supported the society on the grounds of his pro-German feelings and his hatred of Britain. Another individual asserted that they should help the children because Ireland's freedom had been won with German guns.

The tenure of those remarks drew considerable hatred for the Save the German Children Society. Following this meeting the British authorities branded the society fascist and indicated that they would only work with the Irish Red Cross. At the time most of the German children lived in the province of North Rhine Westphalia, which was under British rule.

On 27 July, 1946 88 German children emerged from a passenger ferry and tentatively set foot on Dun Laoghaire pier. The sun dipping into the horizon threw long streaks of blood red into the sky. Waiting for them were a host of Red Cross workers with parcels of food keeping up a stream of conversation, chattering excitedly and laughing. They were accompanied by groups of nervous families who were seeking out the girl or boy who would eventually become their temporary child for next three years.

The German children stared in awe at the treasure trove of cake and fresh fruit as the organisers began the introductions. Among their number was a five-year-old who had been accustomed to a life dominated by the sound of air raid sirens and bomb raids. Then there was seven-year-old Hans Ottengraf, whose father was a prisoner of war in France. Most alarmingly was the spectacle of eight-year-old Elizabeth Kohlberg, who had no idea where she was and shook in terror at the prospect of being sent to a slaughter house. For some, the memory of the horrors of war could never be erased, lingering like an unwelcome visitor, leaving them with an inheritance of quiet despair.

Protestant and Catholic relief agencies in Germany selected children between the ages of five and 15 who were brought here in 1946 and 1947, first to Glencree and later to their temporary homes. Five hundred Christian German children were fostered in this way. It was considered too difficult a task to raise Jewish children in a predominantly Catholic society.

A number of the refugees were orphans, but most had parents who, faced with the consequences of war, could not look after their children. In the heart of Ireland some would learn first hand the bitter truth of Chekov's observation: "For the lonely man the desert is everywhere." They were obviously badly confused by the way they were sent to involuntary exile, but found consolation in the warmth of the welcome.

Some of them would go on to become more Irish than the Irish themselves and were heard to say 'home is home'. This cryptic saying meant that Ireland was far better than all those places you could see on Hollywood films and that the blanket of green in which it wallows, sometimes uncomfortably, was to be preferred to the paved streets of the best cities of the world.

Initially the plan was that these children would remain in Ireland for three years, but such intense bonds were formed that the final departure of refugees led to heart-breaking scenes at Dun Laoghaire and the Government decided that children could stay as long as both the Irish foster parents and their German parents agreed.

A large number of those who left remained in touch with their Irish families. Those who remained here got married and raised Irish families of their own.

Fifty children who came from Germany in 1946 and stayed in Ireland were reunited with those who returned home to Germany during President Herzog's visit in 1997, and relived their memories, including the difficulty of adjusting to a new country and their homesickness. In all 160 of the original 500 foster children and 180 foster families attended. They watched the German president place a commerative plaque and lead a delegation to Glencree, where it all began. They were united inextricably, by a bond which neither fame nor success nor time could destroy. The happiest memories of their lives were shared; memories which had now dimmed the nightmare of those earlier years.

Operation Shamrock is one of the earliest examples of the close ties that began to form between Europe and Ireland after the war, and is an example of the Irish people at their best.

The Scarlet Pimpernel of the Vatican: Msgr Hugh O'Flaherty

I am reliably informed that there are only two types of people – people from Kerry and people who want to be from Kerry! As a big Gaelic football fan I grew up watching the greatest football team of all time – the Kerry team of the 1970s and 1980s. Their players were mythical creatures for me. Such was Kerry's domination of the GAA fields that I associated Kerry simply with great footballers. It came as something of a shock to me to discover in later life that Kerry produced other types of heroes too. On my first visit to Kerry I was introduced to the story of one of the county's most famous sons and to this day I still continue to take inspiration from it.

The late 1930s was a time when Diderot's maxim "only one step separates fanaticism from barbarism" was getting a resounding confirmation in the atrocities of Hitler and Mussolini. During the Second World War, Monsignor Hugh O'Flaherty, better known as the 'Scarlet Pimpernel' of the Vatican, set up an escape organisation for Allied POW's and civilians, which saved over 6,500 lives between 1943-44. His wartime exploits, in which he frequently risked life and limb to hide POWs with Roman friends, were chronicled in a book entitled *The Rome Escape Line,* and a film, *The Scarlet and the Black,* starring Gregory Peck as Msgr O'Flaherty. He was also the subject of a *This Is Your Life* BBC television programme with Eamonn Andrews in 1963.

Born in Lisrobin, Kiskeam, Co. Cork, he studied for the South African missions with the Jesuits in Limerick before moving to Rome, where he was ordained in 1925, after being awarded doctorates in divinity, canon law and philosophy. He was given a post in the Vatican diplomatic service, serving, with a pronounced Kerry accent, in Egypt, Haiti, the Dominican Republic and Czechoslovakia, before returning to Rome in 1938. He cut a dashing figure as he stood on the top steps of the basilica in St Peter's Square, standing, according to his biographer, Sam Derry, "six-foot-two in black soutane, with that utterly Irish rugged face bent over a breviary, glasses glinting on his big nose . . . scanning the square for a familiar figure while murmuring Latin in a Kerry brogue".

One story gives a great insight into his remarkable courage and cleverness in outwitting the Nazis. When he was informed that a British soldier faced imminent arrest and execution he arranged to have him smuggled into Rome under a cartload of cabbages. There the soldier was met by a burly man in black who gazed down from the basilica's left-hand steps and whispered "follow me". The priest led him to a building known as Collegio Teutonico (the German College) which was outside the Vatican, but still on neutral ground. They took refuge in a small bedroom-study, when the priest identified himself: "Make yourself at home. Me name is O'Flaherty and I live here." He thought that a British conspirator should be safe in a place filled with German clergy.

The Irish priest delighted in flirting with danger. Once, after he had stored a British general in a secret hideaway, he took the 'guest' to a Papal reception, dressed in Donegal tweeds, and introduced him as an Irish doctor to the German ambassador.

His exploits as the ex-officio head of the underground British organisation in Rome did not go unnoticed and the German ambassador informed Lieut-Col Herbert Kappler, the Gestapo chief in Rome, that he was the escape line's leader. He was told that if he ever strayed outside the Vatican he would be arrested. A trap was laid to draw him to attend to an injured POW in a village 30 miles from Rome, but at the last second one of his moles revealed that it had been set up by Kappler. After the war O'Flaherty often visited Kappler in prison, baptising him when he converted to Catholicism. The German wrote about O'Flaherty from his cell, "To me he became a fatherly figure".

Shortening the Long Walk to Freedom: Nelson Mandela

Recently I completed the number one item on my bucket list, a visit to Robben Island in Cape Town to see a tiny cell which could have been a cold tomb of loneliness and despair. Inside the sterile, cinder block cell was a toilet, a thin mattress with pillows and a brown blanket. A single window looking into the courtyard has thick, white bars, matching the ones on the door to the cellblock's hallway. Yet while he was a prisoner there, even when little sunlight shone into that cell, Nelson Mandela could see a better future – one worthy of sacrifice. Standing outside that same tiny spot – now a monument to Mandela, where he was incarcerated for 18 years during his long campaign to end the policies of racial apartheid and oppression in his country - was an intense experience.

The emotional impact was accentuated when a few minutes later I and my fellow tourists gathered in a small courtyard where Mandela and other prisoners were forced to work, and where they occasionally played sports. Along one wall stood lattices for grapevines behind which Mandela, while a prisoner, stored his pages of a manuscript that eventually became his acclaimed memoir, *Long Walk to Freedom*. Our guide, who had been a prisoner on Robben Island with Mandela for five years, told us that the pages were smuggled out of the prison. Pointing to a black-and-white photograph of prisoners at work in the courtyard, our guide told us that guards once took away the prisoners' hammers and took pictures to show the world that the inmates were only doing light work. Once the pictures were finished, the hammers were given back.

I read with interest Barack Obama's 2013 comments in the visitor's book, saying that his family was "humbled to stand where men of such courage faced down injustice and refused to yield. The world is grateful for the heroes of Robben Island who remind us that no shackles or cells can match the strength of the human spirit."

He wrote of trying to "transport myself back to those days when President Mandela was still Prisoner 466/64 – a time when the success of his struggle was by no means a certainty. One thing you might not be aware of is that the idea of political non-violence first took root here in South Africa because Mahatma Gandhi was a lawyer here in South Africa. When he we went back to India the principles ultimately led to Indian independence."

Barack Obama, who made the visit with his wife and daughters, called Mandela the ultimate testament to the process of peaceful change and said his daughters now understood his legacy better. "Seeing them stand within the walls that once surrounded Nelson Mandela, I knew this was an experience they would never forget. They appreciate the sacrifices that Madiba (the clan name that many people fondly use to refer to Mandela) and others made for freedom."

The symbolism of Obama's visit to Robben Island was impossible to miss: America's first African-American president, whose wife is a descendant of African slaves, stating publicly that he might not have been elected were it not for Mandela's ability to endure imprisonment and emerge to take power without bitterness or recrimination.

Joseph Conrad wrote that we live as we dream. Mandela lived as he dreamed. He is a prophet calling us to take up the challenge of responding in a practical way to the evils of injustice in all its forms. He dares us to live out the words of Robert Kennedy: "Few will have the greatness to bend history itself, but each of us can work to change a small portion of events. It is from numberless diverse acts of courage and belief that human history is shaped. Each time we stand up for an ideal, or act to improve the lot of others, or strike out against injustice, we send forth a tiny ripple of hope, and crossing each other from a million different centres of energy and daring those ripples build a current which can sweep down the mightiest walls of oppression and resistance."

Holy Wit

"In the beginning was the Word and the Word was No!" This piece of biblical revisionism was penned by Brian Moore and cleverly sums up the experience of those who were brought up to see Christianity, or more precisely Catholicism, in a painfully negative way. That line always returns to me on those frequent occasions when I hear a homily which is couched in purely negative terms.

Recently I attended a special Mass for a group of youngsters. Heroic efforts were made in their preparation with the result that their singing voices sounded nothing less than angelic. Their procession, Prayers of the Faithful and their participation would have charmed the most exacting of liturgists. Their special request was that the Mass should focus on the theme of friendship. But the celebrating priest vetoed their choice of readings and insisted the readings of the day be used.

His seven and a half minute homily contained not one reference to friendship. Instead we were 'treated' to a ranting sermon on the evils that young people today were perpetrating. Sitting at the back of the hall it was fascinating to watch the body language and facial expressions of the congregation - initially everyone sat upright, listening attentively, but as the list of don'ts continued the interest gave way to boredom initially and finally outright antipathy.

Religion should give and enhance life, not drain it. This chapter considers some more life-affirming aspects of the practice of religion. Many people often see religion as a killjoy. This chapter shows that religion can also put a smile on people's faces.

Get an Earful of This

God be in my head and in my understanding;
God be in mine eyes, and in my looking;
God be in my mouth and in my speaking;
God be in my heart, and in my thinking;
God be at mine end, and my departing.
(From the *Sarum Primer,* 1558)

Adventures of the Spirit

I think over again my small adventures
my fears,
those small ones
That I thought so big,
For all the vital things
I had to get and to reach.
And yet there is only one great thing,
The only thing:
To live to see the great day that dawns
And the light that fills the world.
(Native North American song)

We Can Be heroes

In the final scene of the medieval epic *La Chanson de Roland* the great Christian hero Charlemagne sat exhausted in Aix, his battles with the Moors over. According to the poem, he was more than 900 years old. An angel woke the old man from his sleep and told him to get up again and return to battle, because the work would not be finished until the end of time. Charlemagne sighed: *Dieu, si penuse est ma vie.* (O God how hard is my life) "The work of the hero remains unfinished but who will do it if not he?"

The Origin of the Species

Teacher: "Who lived in the garden of Eden?"
Young pupil: "The Adams family!"

Bellyache

The teacher was explaining the biblical story of Jonah and the whale to the class when she asked: "Now tell me, what does that story tell us?" One little girl said: "You can't keep a good man down."

Go With the Crowd

A visiting preacher was greeted at the end of the Sunday service with the frank appraisal of one worshipper: "That was the worst sermon I ever heard. It was complete nonsense!"

The visiting preacher, quite disturbed, informed the resident vicar of what the man had said. The vicar replied: "That poor chap is not really responsible for what he says. He never has an original thought. He just goes around repeating what everybody else is saying!"

On a Wing and a Prayer

The ship was sinking rapidly and the captain was nervously passing out the life-jackets. He shouted out: "Does anyone here know how to pray?" Immediately a man said: "I do."

The captain replied: "Thank goodness for that, we're short one life-jacket!"

Four-ever and Ever

Teacher: "How many wives can a man have?"
Francis: "Sixteen."
Teacher: "Where did you hear that?"
Francis: "The priest at the wedding said: four better, four worse, four richer, four poorer."

A Helpful Hint

Following rigidly the monastic rules whereby one must not complain about one's food, a young monk found a mouse in his soup, so he attracted the attention of the server. "Please Brother! The monk next to me has no mouse in his soup."

Parking Problems

During rush hour traffic a lawyer in San Francisco, having driven around a court building for a place to park, finally drove up onto a pavement outside a church with a 'No Parking' sign nearby. He left a note: "Drove around for 30 minutes, forgive us our trespasses" and a $10 dollar bill for good measure. Some time later he went back to his car, only to find a note and his money still there, accompanied by a parking ticket and a note which read: "Been a cop for 30 years. Lead us not into temptation."

Psalm 23 Revisited

The Lord is my intimate friend, I want for nothing.
He sits down with me and puts my heart at rest.
He eats my simple meal with me and this gives me joy.
Like a true friend he listens to all my trials and tribulations.
In times of heartbreak he comforts me.
Whenever tears topple down my cheeks he dries them away.
When I walk in the valley of darkness,
he takes me gently by the hand whenever I'm in danger
of collapsing,
and gives me the strength to go on.
Whenever I'm on the point of exhaustion,
he revives me with a cool drink.
When I am hungry he provides me with food,
he shares with wanton abandon.
As I walk on my heart soars with joy,
because his eye roams constantly on me,
even if I seem to be lost in the crowd.
I know he will hear my plea above the din,
like a mother knows her own child's cry.
When my earthly journey is over,
I will begin again.
He will take me to his home,
my home,
and we'll supper together at the table he has prepared for me.

A Grave Matter

Notice outside cemetery: "Due to an employee' strike this cemetery will be maintained by a skeleton staff.'"

The Wood from the Trees

The rector had a wooden leg. One day he was in such a terrible hurry that he parked his car on a double yellow line. Hoping to avoid a parking ticket, he wrote a message for the warden on his windscreen: "Have pity - wooden leg." He returned to find both a ticket and a note: "No pity - wooden heart!"

The Bitter Truth

A woman went to confession saying, "Father I was looking into a mirror and I decided I was beautiful. Was this is a terrible sin?" The priest answered: "Certainly not. It was just a terrible mistake."

At the Cutting Edge

During Sunday service the preacher explained in the course of a long-winded sermon why he had a plaster on his face: "I was concentrating so much on my homily this morning, that while shaving, I cut myself." After the service as he was counting the money in the collection plate he discovered a note which read: "In future, reverend, concentrate on the shaving and cut the sermon!"

Caught Out

Edward Kennedy told of a lecturer at a theological college who informed his class that the subject of his next lecture would be the sin of deceit and that, by way of preparation, he would like them all to read the seventeenth chapter of St Mark's Gospel. When the lecture began, he asked how many had compiled with his instructions. Most of them raised their hands: "Thank you," said the lecturer. "It is to people like you that today's lecture is especially addressed. There is no seventeenth chapter in Mark's Gospel."

Mission Impossible

After 40 days the flood finally subsided, Noah opened all the doors of the ark and the animals walked out two by two - all except the snakes.

"Why don't you go out and multiply?" said Noah.

"We can't," groaned one of the snakes, "You see, we're adders."

Religious Convictions

Prison chaplain: "Why are you back here again, Thomas?"
Thomas: "Because of my belief, sir."
Chaplain: "What? How could your belief bring you back to prison?"
Thomas: "I happened to believe that the policeman had already patrolled his beat past the bank."

On the Spot

The professor was speaking of the wisdom of the Proverbs in the scriptures when a student spoke up: "I think there's nothing remarkable in the proverbs. They are rather commonplace remarks of common people."

"Okay," said the professor, "Make one."

Prayer for Good Humour

....

Grant me, O Lord, good digestion, and also something to digest.
Grant me a healthy body, and the necessary good humour
to maintain it.
Grant me a simple soul that knows to treasure all that is
good and that doesn't frighten easily at the sight of evil,
but rather finds the means to put things back in their place.
Give me a soul that knows not boredom, grumblings,
sighs and laments,
nor excess of stress, because of that obstructing thing
called 'I'.
Grant me, O Lord, good sense of humour.
Allow me the grace to be able to take a joke, to discover in
life a bit of joy, and to be able to share it with others.
St Thomas More

Holy Mother

Traditionally in Ireland we welcomed the fine weather by joining the rush to erect a May altar in honour of Our Lady. Boxes, tea-chests and all kinds of idle implements were draped with white sheets to make homemade altars. Flowers were piled into jam jars for decorations. The most colourful ceremony of all was the procession from the chapel down to the village. It seemed to be an injunction for the sacred to leave the church and make its home in the ordinary. Every house along the way was decorated with flowers. From an early age we were taught a great devotion for the Virgin Mary - intercessor, mother of mercy, star of the sea. To call upon the father for daily bread and praise the kingdom, the power and the glory, was inspiring and comforting, but we felt a warm glow within us when we spoke phrases like "fruit of thy womb".

Mary was an integral part of the fabric of Irish life, even Irish history. One story told was about the Virgin Mary walking by a house in the West of Ireland on a stormy night during the Great Famine. She and the child Jesus had no coat to protect them from the elements. As they passed the house, the woman of the house called them inside and gave Mary a bowl of nettle soup, and an old sack to give extra cover to the child. Mary's final blessing was that the family line would always remain intact. They were one of the few families who survived the Great Hunger. A sign that God's favour rested on them was that their rooster did not crow 'cockadoodle-doo' but rather cried out, "The Virgin's Son is risen."

Two for the Show

Bitter experience has taught me that if someone wants to find fault with you they will. It is a bit like the story of the garda sergeant, a total so and so, who was on his last day in the town before he retired from the force. He was a mean and spiteful man, and had 'caught' everyone in the town for some offence or other. The only person who had escaped was the parish priest. The garda was determined to rectify that situation on his last day. He knew that the priest always cycled home after saying morning Mass so the garda stood at the bottom of the hill. His plan had been to step out in front of the priest, forcing him to swerve and topple over and then he could 'do him' for dangerous driving. He carried out his plan but although the priest swerved he kept control of his bike. The priest stopped though to wish the garda well on his retirement. The cop said: "Jesus, you were fierce lucky not to fall then."

The priest replied, "Indeed I was lucky but then I had God with me."

The garda nearly danced for joy as he said, "I'm doing you for having two on a bike."

The Quality of Mercy

Religion was a powerful influence for good and for bad early in my life. I often think of a saying attributed to Gandhi when he said, "I like your Christ. I do not like your Christians. Your Christians are not like your Christ." I suppose for me, listening to and observing people, it seems we are great at talking it but not great living it. I remain a great believer in the philosophy of Christianity. What we need are people to live it.

When Pope John XXIII was a cardinal, one night he was sitting down for his supper in Venice and his secretary came in with the file of a priest who was in trouble. The assistant was very disdainful as he spoke about the priest who was having a bad time. The Pope pointed at his glass on the table and asked his secretary who it belonged to. "You own it, your Eminence," replied the puzzled secretary. Then the pope picked up the glass and threw it on the ground where it smashed into smithereens. "Who owns it now?"

"You still own it, your Eminence."

"And I still own that priest too," said the Pope.

Adieu

A vicar and his curate did not see eye-to-eye. The vicar arranged that, the bane of his life would be transferred to another parish. Before the curate left he asked the vicar to attend his final service. Somewhat surprised, the senior clergyman agreed. The curate's homily consisted of just one sentence: "Tarry ye here with the ass while I go yonder."

Thieves in the Night

Fifteen churches have been closed in Dublin because of swindling congregations.

Report in *The Evening Herald.*

Mathematical Problems

Why weren't there only 10 apostles if God intended us to decimalise?
Why do people who don't believe in miracles buy lottery tickets?

Revisionism

....

Some years ago a cynic presented his religious education teacher with an alternative view of 12 traditional dogmas.

1. The Bible is a prophet and lust account.
2. A Catholic is one who commits more sins than anybody else but gets no fun out of it.
3. A Church bazaar is a fete worse than death.
4. Love is a temporary insanity curable by marriage.
5. The sacrament of marriage represents a woman's effort to transform a night owl into a homing pigeon.
6. Martyrdom is the only way you can become famous without talent.
7. Morals are what you have before someone discovers the truth about you.
8. Prayer is a little message sent to God last thing at night to get the cheaper rate.
9. Puritanism is the haunting fear that someone, somewhere, might just be happy.
10. A saint is someone who's hell to live with.
11. A sceptic is one who lost his wallet in a church while standing between a policeman and a nun.
12. Sunday School is a prison in which children do penance for the guilty conscience of their parents.

Situation Not Vacant

Once there was a rumour that George Bernard Shaw was thinking of becoming a Catholic. A friend asked him if there was any truth in it.
"Certainly not," said Shaw. "They've already got a Pope."

Labourers in the Vineyard

Reporter: "How many people work in the Vatican?"
Pope John XXIII: "Oh, about half of them."

No-Go Area

"In no circumstances shall a priest who wears trousers ever be allowed to occupy a pulpit."
Taken from the 1820 Trust Deed of a Kent non-conformist chapel.

Substitute

"A large crowd attended the Palm Sunday service. The donkey failed to arrive for the procession at St Peter's Church, so that the procession was led by Fr Lee instead." Report in parish bulletin.

Through the Eyes of a child

A Sunday School teacher got some radical insights into theology from some of her students:
"The bishop wears a meter on his head to increase his offerings."
"When a woman is married to just one man that's what's called monotony."
"Insects is burned in some churches."
"An epistle is the wife of an apostle."
"A fast day is when you have to eat in a hurry."
"The Angus Dei is a lady composer of music."
"Joan of Arc was married to Noah."

To Speed on Angels' Wings

An angel in Heaven was welcoming a new arrival. "And tell me how did you get here?" she asked.
The new angel replied, "Flu."

The Lord Knows

A keen fan of the acclaimed poet Robert Browning asked him what he meant by a particular image in one of his poems. "When I wrote it," Browning replied, "only two people knew the significance - myself and God. Now only God knows."

Red Alert

A young girl was listening to a very boring sermon. Suddenly her eye was caught by the red sanctuary lamp. Tugging at her mother's sleeve she asked, "Mammy, when the light turns green can we go?"

Yours Sin-cerely

"Miss Hampshire has fine, fair skin, which she admits comes out in a mass of freckles at the first hint of sin." Evening newspaper headline

Once Bitten Twice Shy

A renowned preacher returned home from a trip one morning with such a tiny amount of change in his pocket that he gave his last penny to the porter. Forgetting this when he was approached by a tramp at the bus station, he invited the down-and-out, with characteristic generosity, to dine with him for breakfast in the local restaurant.

After a slap-up-meal, the preacher got on his feet to pay the bill only to discover there was nothing in his pocket. The tramp, seeing his predicament, paid for both of them.

Mortified with embarrassment, the preacher said: "Come with me in a taxi to my home and I will pay you back."

"No way," replied the tramp. "You've caught me for a meal, but there's no way you're getting a taxi fare out of me as well."

New Recruit

At the end of a very long and uninspiring homily the priest announced that he wished to meet the Board of Parishioners in the sacristy after Mass. When it came time for the meeting, the priest noticed a strange face there.
"You're not a member of the board," he said.
To which the man in question replied, "I certainly am - I was never more bored in my life!"

Unfit for Publication

The bishop came to the town to address a gathering. He began by making a request to reporters that as he was making the same speech the following week in a neighbouring town, could they refrain from publishing it. The following day he was horrified to read in the local paper, "Bishop Jones delivered an excellent lecture - he told some wonderful stories - unfortunately they cannot be printed."

Lady's Choice

A parishioner had been very faithful in attending all her church's services for many years, and the vicar wanted to reward her. At the beginning of the next Sunday's service he announced, "For her loyalty to the church we shall reward Miss Hoey by letting her pick a hymn for the evening."

"Oh goody," exclaimed Miss Hoey, and pointing to a member of the congregation, she said, "I'll take him."

The Camera Never Lies

A well-known but very cantankerous bishop was having his photograph taken by a press cameraman. The photographer had a lot of trouble trying to get his subject to pose properly. Eventually, after much bickering, he was about to take the picture.

"Look pleasant for a moment," said the photographer. "Then you can be yourself again."

A Little Morsel

"Now, Kitty," the parish priest said to his housekeeper, "When Archbishop O'Connell arrives you must say 'Your Grace'."

The bell rang precisely at the appointed time. Kitty hurried to the door, opened it, looked at the archbishop and solemnly said: "Bless us, O Lord, and these thy gifts, which of thy bounty we are about to receive, through Christ our Lord. Amen."

All Ends Up

"The priest announced last Sunday that he was going to install a second font near the channel steps, so that he could baptise babies at both ends."

Excerpt from magazine article on baptism.

Hellish Choir

Rev Francis was in a hurry one Saturday and consequently did not give as much attention to the layout of the church noticeboard as normal. The next morning the choir were a bit miffed to see his injunction to "Come hear our choir" immediately under the title of his sermon 'What Is Hell Like?'

Career Move

"And why did you leave your last job?" Fr Roberts asked the young applicant for the position of parish secretary.
"It was something the boss said," came the reply.
"Was he abusive to you?" asked Fr Roberts in a voice full of concern.
"No, not really."
"Well then, what did he say?"
"He said, 'You're fired'."

Angel Eyes

Wealthy businessman Michael MacGrath and his teenage daughter were driving to town in his new car.
"Be an angel, Dad," said his daughter, "and let me drive!"
He did. And he is.

Identity Test

A man arrived in the vicarage in great distress. He had just been assaulted.

"Can you describe your assailant?" Rev Hardy asked as he handed the man a cup of tea.

"Of course I can! That's what I was doing when he hit me."

Sense and Sensitivity

Some years ago a story in the newspapers appeared about a wayward minister of the Anglican Church. The then Archbishop of Canterbury, Dr Runcie, was asked to comment on the incident. He simply said: "In this earthly tabernacle there are many mansions and they are all made of glass." Dr Runcie was highlighting the importance of compassion and sensitivity in human relationships.

Constancy?

Liverpool signed Avi Cohen and made him the first Israeli international to play for the reds. Avi's mother was a devout member of the Jewish faith and was concerned that Avi would lose out on his faith in Liverpool. A few weeks after he arrived in the club she rang her son and said, "Do you still wear your skull cap?"

Avi: "No one wears skull caps in Liverpool."

Mrs Cohen: "Do you still go the synagogue on the Sabbath?"

Avi: "How can I? We have a match every Saturday."

Mrs Cohen [attributed]: "Tell me, are you still circumcised?"

Crocodile Dundee

Even the Scottish clergy react to Scottish victories over England. A famous example of their holy wit is a story set in darkest Africa, where there was a river infested with crocodiles. On the other side there was a tribe which various missionaries wanted to convert. However, nobody was willing to take the risk of crossing the river. In 2018 along came a group of missionary priests from Dundee who waded across the river without coming to any harm. Shortly after they revealed their secret. "We wore t-shirts bearing the words England - World Cup Champions 2018.

And sure not even a crocodile was willing to swallow that!"

Died in Service

One Sunday morning, the pastor noticed little Gavin Peacock was staring up at the large plaque that hung in the foyer of the church. It was covered with names, and small flags were mounted on either side of it. The seven-year-old had been staring at the plaque for some time, so the pastor walked up, stood beside the boy, and said quietly, "Good morning Gavin".

"Good morning pastor," replied the young Gavin, still focused on the plaque, then he asked, "What is this?"

"Well, son, it's a memorial to all the young men and women who died in the service."

Soberly, they stood together, staring at the large plaque. Little Gavin's voice was barely audible when he asked, "Which service, the 9.45 or the 11.15?"

A Discerning Eye

Taking advantage of a balmy day in Newcastle, Alan Shearer donned his polos and khakis for a game of golf. Before he teed off, he watched four men produce some really horrible shots. After 20 minutes watching the foursome Alan asked, "You guys wouldn't be priests by any chance?"

"Actually, yes, we are," one cleric replied, "How did you know?"

"Easy. I've never seen such bad golf and such clean language."

The One in the Mirror

A new priest in a small parish spent the first few months of his ministry calling on his parishioners to be actively involved in the parish. But they would hardly turn up to any of his services. Desperate, one day he placed a notice in the local newspaper stating that as the parish was dead, it was his duty to give it a decent burial.

The funeral would be held on the following weekend. Morbidly curious, the whole parish turned out. At the front of the church, they saw a high coffin smothered in flowers. The preacher carried out his funeral rites in the usual way and preached a homily; then he invited his congregation to step forward and pay their last respects to the dearly beloved who had departed.

The long line filed by. Each mourner peeped into the coffin and turned away with a guilty, sheepish look for, in the coffin, titled at the correct angle was a large mirror. Everyone saw themselves.

5

All in the Game?

Sport teaches us the power of community instead of the power of one. It teaches us that we need to expand our minds and embrace a vision in which the group imperative takes precedence over individual glory: to move from thinking about 'me' to thinking about 'we' - because the most crucial lesson sport teaches us is that selflessness is the key. There is no me in team. In this chapter we see some parables of sport – and life – at its best.

All I Had to Do was Dream

As a boy my childhood ambition was to play football for Roscommon. My first chance came at the age of 11 when I was picked to play for Saint Brigids under-12s in Knockcroghery. When we got there the dressing room was locked, so we had to tog out in the field next door – which was a graveyard. It was to be a real metaphor for my football career!

Things did not go well for the team but I was really happy with my performance because I was playing corner-back and any time the ball came into my direction I was first out, cleared it and my man never got a touch of the ball. At half-time we gathered for what I hoped would be an inspirational speech from our manager who was the local parish priest. As he was God's ambassador on Earth I was more than a little surprised when he came into the circle and grabbed me by the jersey, with his face red, his eyes almost popping out of his head, the veins of his neck bulging like crazy and flecks of his spit flying all over my face as he spoke.

All he said was "They're bleeping killing ye". Then he let me go and told me he was taking me off. The first half was not great but the second half was even – it was even worse! We lost narrowly. The final score was 7 goals and 21 points to 2 points. The guy I had been marking was on fire in the second half and destroyed us. To this day I still can't understand why I was taken off. I really think it is the kind of injustice that Amnesty International should consider taking on.

Anyway, my ambition of playing for Roscommon died that day. Some time later the Olympics were on TV and one night I saw the late Jimmy Magee talking so lyrically about one of the guys that was representing Ireland in shooting that I decided to start watching the shooting competition, and then my new ambition became to represent Ireland at the Olympics in shooting.

The following Sunday I went to my uncle's house and asked him to teach me how to shoot. His best friend was with him and they brought me out into the back garden to begin my induction to sporting immortality. This was a time when people had their dinner in the middle of the day. And our idea of a varied diet was that three days a week we had cabbage and bacon and the next three days we had bacon and cabbage. But if we were lucky on a Sunday we had a tin or two of peas. So my uncle explained to me the basics of shooting and put three empty tins of Bachelor peas on the wall. He then took aim and shot one of the tins off the wall. His friend did the same, with the same result. So there was just one left for me. I took the gun, closed my eyes and fired.

With the benefit of hindsight it might not have been the smartest move in the world for me to close my eyes before I fired the shot – but this time the tin of peas stood unmoved. I was crestfallen. Then I looked at my uncle and I could not understand why he suddenly looked pale. Then I saw he was looking about 30 yards to the left where the clothes line was. There was just one item on the clothes line – which was his good shirt. And now this lovely white shirt had a great big hole in it – and ugly black smoke was emanating from it.

Two consequences of that episode were – my ambition to shoot for Ireland in the Olympics died there and then.

And my uncle has been shirty with me ever since!

Me and Jimmy Magee

In the pantheon of Irish sport special place is reserved for the late, great Jimmy Magee. No less a diplomat than a great broadcaster, he had a great flair for handling Leeds United fans. 'Jimmy', an anxious Leeds fan desperately seeking assurance enquired, "do you think we still have a great team?"

"Ah, my good man," Jimmy replied with the utmost sincerity, "'Great' is not the word to describe it!"

They say confession is good for the soul. I hope so. For over 30 years I have harboured a dark secret from my family. Many's the sleepless night I have turned and twisted in my bed as the pangs of guilt racked my troubled conscience. No amount of counting sheep could shake off the tidal waves of remorse that swept over me.

In my defence, it wasn't really my fault. The real villain was Jimmy Magee. The great sports commentators share a magical capacity to raise and refresh the spirit and to heighten the quality of human perception. Jimmy Magee was one of them. His was a world of wonder, admiration and enchantment.

It was the 1979 FA Cup final and my only worry was if Liam Brady would lead Arsenal to triumph over Manchester United. My family though were in a tizzy because my aunt Sheila was getting married two days later after a 12-year courtship. Nobody could accuse her of marrying in haste. The match had thankfully permitted me to provide a pretext for missing the rehearsal. All I had to do was deposit the newly acquired three-tiered wedding cake into my uncle-in-law-to-be's car while the rest of the family went to the church.

With five minutes to go Arsenal were cruising with a 2-0 lead and Jimmy assured me that the match was theirs. This was the moment to leave out the cake.

It was starting to rain. The rain slid, tapping, through the branches, and swept in windy puffs across the fields. As I carefully placed the cake on the back seat of William's capri I could hear Jimmy recklessly abandoning his normal calm, mellifluous tones for a state of near frenzy. I raced back inside to see that United had scored. Jimmy could scarcely contain his excitement. A minute later United equalised. Jimmy's voice pulsated with enthusiasm. Then with time almost up Chippy Brady produced another piece of wizardry to sensationally set up the winning goal. By now Jimmy was in a state of near mystical rapture.

At the final whistle a feeling of panic descended on me. I raced outside. My worst fears were realised. I had left the car door open and our dog - imaginatively called Lassie - was licking the wedding cake.

Lassie was warm, brown and smooth-coated, with a cream arrow on her forehead and flecks of cream on her two front feet. She was a very knowing, friendly creature and I loved her with a passion. At that moment I could have killed her, especially as icing dripped off her whiskers like a snowman melting in a heatwave.

The damage to the cake was surprisingly small and a little surgery with a knife seemed to do the trick.

Blood may be thicker than water, but it is also a great deal nastier. I decided that news of Lassie's appreciation for the wedding cake was best kept to myself. Whoever said silence is golden knew what they were talking about.

Such was my acute anxiety that overnight I was attacked by a virulent form of acne. My mother thought that was the reason that during the wedding I sought the shadows as resolutely as the Phantom of the Opera.

A look of adoration passed into my aunt's face as she cut the cake, like the look of the mother of a child who has just won first prize. To my eyes the icing looked as buttery and soft as white custard. So acute was the sensation of panic across my chest I felt I might explode.

Everyone agreed they had never tasted nicer wedding-cake.

When In Rome

For people of a certain age, Ireland's first appearance in the World Cup soccer finals in Italy in 1990 was a kind of Golden Age. It was like an adult version of Christmas as the nation held its breath and Ireland qualified for the quarter-finals. Rermarkably the tournament produced an unlikey national icon – the team's English manager Jack Charlton. Eamon Dunphy apart, the nation appeared to be under his spell. After the tournament was over I resolved to get an interview with big Jack. It took over two years and a lot of resilience but eventually I got the thumbs up from the great man.

The first thing you notice when you meet Jack Charlton for the first time is the speed with which he forgets your name. The conversation about football is peppered with comments like 'the boy with the great left foot' and 'that nippy little winger' which substitute for players names. In Jack's distinctive Geordie brogue most becomes 'moost' and goalkeeper becomes 'gullkeepah'.

One of the consequences of Ireland's qualification for the quarter-finals of Italia '90 was the trip to Rome and the opportunity to meet the Pope - an experience Charlton said he will treasure forever.

"I have to say it was a slightly tense occasion for me. I am not a Catholic so I found the ceremonial aspect a bit of puzzling. We always had a priest in to say Mass for the Irish team and I attended those, but an event with the Pope is something completely different and a very big deal.

"I didn't know when to go forward and when to go back

so I didn't want to embarrass myself or anybody else by making a cock-up. I knew it was a very proud moment for the players and all the staff. For some of them it would be the icing on the cake of probably the biggest event of their football lives but for others it would be the biggest event of their lives. The only thing was the ceremony went on and on because there were so many delegations there and the Pope welcomed them in many different languages. It was also very hot and I was petrified I would nod off and be shown in every newspaper in the world falling asleep when I was meeting the Pope!

"No matter what your religion is the Vatican is a mighty organisation. The Pope is a very charismatic man, if I can use the word. He is someone that you would like to meet regardless of your own beliefs. He said to me: 'Ah Mr Charlton. The boss.' It was nice to bring a Catholic team to see the Pope. I have pictures at home showing me meeting him. I am very happy with those photos."

I was afraid Big Jack would choke with laughter when I suggested that he would be canonised by the Irish people because of the success he has achieved with the team.

"Public attention is part of the job. I'm a miner's son from the North East of England who spent a life in football. They gave me a job to do which was to produce a team which would get results and bring people into the game. I was very successful in doing exactly that. The fact that the people of Ireland like me is great. I like being popular. I would be a liar if I said I didn't. It's got its drawbacks. There is very little privacy anymore. Canonisation? You couldn't do that to me - I'm a Protestant!"

I conducted my interview with Big Jack in a hotel room in Dublin when he was just out of the shower. All he was wearing was a bathrobe - which was a little too revealing for my comfort. Not wanting to delay the great man unnecessarily, when we had finished our chat I hastily gathered together my recording gear. Too hastily, because when I got outside I discovered I had unwittingly taken one of his stockings. I had a major moral dilemma immediately: who else could say they had a souvenir of Jack Charlton's sock? Catholic guilt got the better of me though and I returned it – much to Jack's amusement.

My one consolation is that I got closer than any other reporter to the sole of Jack Charlton.

A Nun's Story

Packie Bonner was goalkeeper with Celtic in the 1980s and 1990s and will always be a national icon in Ireland because of that famous penalty save in Italia '90. Packie had the prayers of the fans backing him. One woman took it to extremes. She lit a candle and put it over the place on the television set that Packie occupied. Then she changed it in the second half when Packie changed positions to ensure that it would be burning over his head.

Packie's status as one of the top goalies in the world did not come without a price. He attracted huge adulation from people of all ages - including nuns. He went into hospital for a hernia operation. He had missed Mass on the Sunday and because he was in the Bon Secours - a nun's hospital - it was a very holy place. He thought he would go to Mass during the week, so he went down to the 10 o'clock service. It was all nuns except himself. He was being very holy that day. In most churches people leave as soon as the priest is finished, but he made sure he was not going to make that mistake, and decided to stay as long as the nuns. As the priest said his final little bit, a little nun came up beside him and said, "Excuse me Mr Bonner I wonder if you could sign my Bible for me?" Packie's sure she is still doing penance somewhere for that!

Another time during his Celtic days he was in hospital for the cup final and Celtic were playing. He was all set to watch the match on television when a nun from an enclosed order came in to see him and sat down on the chair. She stood chatting to him for the whole afternoon. He had to switch off the telly and missed the whole match.

SOS

....

As winds raged at 35 knots and played havoc with sailing boats during the sailing competition at Punsan during the Seoul Olympics in 1988, two sailors of the Singapore team, Joseph Chan and Shaw Her, were thrown overboard when their boat capsised.

Lawrence Lemieux of Canada was sailing alone in the silver medal position in a separate event when he saw the sailors in distress. The Canadian rushed to Chan, who was exhausted from struggling against the strong currents in his heavy sailing jacket. By the time Lemieux had completed his rescue attempt, he had lagged way behind in his race.

However, the Olympic ideal was revived when the judges awarded Lemieux second place. Moreover, the International Olympic committee presented him with a special award for his gallantry.

Asked about his heroism Lemieux simply said, "It's the first rule of sailing to help people in distress."

Days of Grace

....

Racial prejudice, social injustice, tennis, courage, three heart attacks and AIDS were the currents of a rich fruit cake which made up the life of Arthur Ashe.

He first made his mark in 1960 when he won his first title - the US National Junior Indoor Championship. On the professional circuit he made an immediate impression. In the final of the 1968 US Open, he served 26 aces and beat Holland's Tom Okker. It was the first time a black man had won one of tennis' four major tournaments.

In 1970 he won another, the Australian Open; in 1971 he won the French Open doubles title with his partner Marty Riessen and in 1975 he defeated reigning champion Jimmy Connors to claim the Wimbledon title. He was twice ranked number one in the world. Arthur also played on four Davis Cup championship teams, and captained the team to titles in 1981 and 1982.

He had his first heart attack at the age of 36. He underwent bypass surgery then and again four years later. As recovery from his second operation was particularly slow, he agreed to receive a few extra units of blood as a boost. Five years later, his right hand went limp. Emergency surgery revealed the cause: AIDS.

Resilience was his trademarks, as was evident in his childhood when his mother died. His father sat on his son's bed, weeping as he told him the news. The boy answered, "Don't cry, Daddy. As long as we have each other we'll be all right." This same resilience was also evident in his final days.

After keeping his illness a secret he went public about it in April 1992, when he learned that a newspaper intended to print a story about his condition. Despite being weak from the illness, he continued his lifelong work helping children, working to give haven to Haitian refugees, fighting racial injustice and battling AIDS. Right up to the very end he maintained that the biggest problem he had to endure in life was not AIDS, but racial prejudice.

Throughout his adult life he fought to bring blacks and whites together. In 1973 he broke the colour line on the courts of South Africa, a country he often visited both to meet black leaders and to visit the youth of Soweto. He was arrested for protesting against apartheid and successfully worked to have South Africa banned from the Davis Cup.

Asked before he died if he felt cheated, he answered, "Death doesn't frighten me. If I asked 'Why me?' about my troubles, I would have to ask 'Why me?' about my blessings. Why my winning Wimbledon? Why my marrying a beautiful, gifted woman and having a wonderful child?"

Sportsmanship

....

The essential thing is not to have conquered but to have fought well.

Nowhere was this Olympic ideal better captured than at the 1964 Winter Olympics in Innsbruck. Italy's Eugenio Monti and Sergio Siorapes were hot favourites to win gold in the two-man bobsleigh event. But as they awaited their second run, the rank outsiders of Tony Nash and Robin Nixon of the British team were feeling at the bottom of the world. Following a sensational first run, their sleigh had broken an axle bolt and it seemed inevitable that they would have to withdraw from the competition.

Monti had completed his second run and, seeing the predicament of his opponents, immediately stripped the bolt from his own sleigh and offered it to Nash. In one of the most dramatic upsets in the history of the competition, the British went on to win the gold while the Italians only received the bronze.

Justice was given four years later when Monti drove both his two- and four-man sleds to Olympic victory.

A Baron and a Gentleman

Throughout its history the Davis Cup Competition has produced many colourful characters, such as the Australian Mark Kratzmann who learned to play tennis on a court made of flattened anthills. However, no man typifies the true spirit of the Davis Cup more than the German Baron Gottfried von Cramm. In the 1937 semi-final in which America fought a titanic battle against the Germans, von Cramm faced Don Budge with the matches tied at 2-2 to decide the result. In the prevailing Nazi fervour the German was told to win it for 'The Fatherland'.

The sets went 2-2 and in the deciding fifth von Cramm took a 4-1 game lead. Budge pulled back to draw 4-4. The German took the lead again until the American levelled at 6-6. The German saved five match points as dusk fell before the American eventually won. Despite his disappointment, von Cramm was smiling when he came to the net and warmly congratulated his opponent on his magnificent play. The Americans went on to win the cup and a few months later the Nazis arrested von Cramm on trumped-up charges. He was locked in jail for seven months before being drafted into the German army. However, in 1951 he played in the Davis Cup again at the age of 42.

The other incident he is best remembered for in the competition was when he teamed up in a vital doubles match with Kai Lund. Towards the end of the game both Germans lunged for the ball at the same time. Lund hit the ball for a winner, and the umpire called game, set and match for Germany. Signalling in protest, von Cramm said his racket had touched ball and the point was lost. The match resumed but the German pair lost. Subsequently the German crowd accused von Cramm of letting his country down. His reply: "I think I'm doing them credit."

One Woman and her Horse

Twenty-three-year-old Lisa Hartel, Denmark's leading equestrienne, was expecting her first child when she awoke one morning with a headache and a stiff neck in 1944. She was soon to hear the devastating news that she was the victim of polio.

Nonetheless, she was determined to still represent Denmark in international competition. Bit by bit she learned to lift her arm, then she regained the use of her thigh muscles. Miraculously, she went on to have a healthy daughter and both mother and daughter learned to crawl together.

A year later Lisa was able to walk using crutches. Slowly she began to literally find her feet.

In 1952 she was chosen to represent her native country at the Helsinki Olympics. She became the first woman to take a medal in an equestrian event when she won the silver medal in the individual dressage. When gold medallist Henri St Cyr helped her onto the victory platform, it was one of the great sporting moments - a magnificent triumph of the human spirit in the face of enormous adversity.

Simplicity is Genius

When Lee Trevino was winning one of his most famous golf tournaments, the TV coverage picked up on the fact that he kept looking at one of his gloves and the fact that he had a word scribbled on it which was indistinguishable. After he won the tournament he was bombarded with questions from the media about the word and he told them that it was the word 'Kiss'. They were all confused by his response so he explained that it stood for: 'Keep It Simple Stupid'.

Without the Spin

Today, in sport as in some many areas of life, everything is spun to sell a message rather than to convey the truth. Ernest Shackleton's recruiting advertisement for his 1912 Imperial Trans-Antarctic Expedition was: "Men wanted for hazardous journey. Small wages, bitter cold, long months of complete darkness, constant danger, safe return doubtful. Honour and recognition in case of success."

If Shackleton were advertising today he would have said: "Members wanted for adventure trek. Low cost, cool sights, lots of fun nights, thrills galore, insurance available. Get your picture in *Outdoor* magazine."

The Lesser Known Miracle

Claude Stevens won the silver medal at the discus at the Montreal Disabled Athletes Olympics. Claude was a merchant seaman for 20 years until he fell off the hold of a ship and was paralysed from the chest down. He was renowned for his sense of humour. One of his favourite stories was of the wheelchair athlete who flew to Lourdes for a cure, but was so exhausted when he got there that they were afraid to take him out of the wheelchair to immerse him in the pool, as is the traditional practice for pilgrims, for fear he might collapse. Instead they put him, wheelchair and all, into the sacred pool. Then another of the great Lourdes miracles took place. The man was not cured, but when he came out the wheelchair had a new set of tyres!

History makers

Good habits are learned young. As a boy, legendary cricketer Brian Lara learned to bat using a scrunched-up evaporated milk can as the ball. If he missed it, it cut his leg. He didn't miss very often.

Glory Days

....

When Japan invaded Korea in 1910 they immediately attempted to quash the indigenous Korean culture. The only avenue the Koreans had to compete on equal terms with their conquerors was on the running track.

Sohn Kee Chung was a young runner who trained hard along the banks of the Yalu River, with sand in his trousers and stones on his back. But the only way he could win anything was under the flag of the despised Japanese. In 1936 he won the Japanese marathon trials. Reluctantly, they were forced to send him to the Berlin games but they tried to curtail the damage by giving him a Japanese name, Kitei Son. But when he signed in, he did so using his Korean name.

Sohn won the race in Olympic record time. At the medal ceremony, when the Japanese flag was raised, he bowed his head in protest.

It was not until 1988 that he could adequately celebrate his achievement when, as a 76-year-old, he entered the Seoul stadium bearing the Olympic torch. In a moment that brought tears to the entire crowd, Sohn bounded around the track, leaping for joy like a child and bursting with pride for himself and his country.

The Terrible Twins

To this day I still don't know why Joe and Jim were called 'the terrible twins'. Okay they really were twins, that still does not explain the 'terrible'.

What really puzzles me though is the genetic aberration that could have produced two people who were so totally unlike in every conceivable way as brothers, let alone twins. Jim was a young version of Robert Redford. Joe looked like he was born to play the baddie in a James Bond movie. Jim was outgoing, gregarious and carefree. Joe was reserved and had a vulnerability about him and a sadness that clung to him. He left a sense that his mind often travelled in a land uninhabited by the rest of us. During school term Jim seemed to live outside the gates of the local convent school, but Joe wouldn't be caught dead there.

The contrast between the two brothers was most evident on the football field. From the ages of 12 to 14 Jim was spoken of as the most promising player seen in Roscommon since Dermot Earley. In full flight he was a sight to put a permanent tingle in the blood, with his swashbuckling solo runs which cut through opposing defences like a knife through butter. His exceptional ability was matched only by his complete lack of dedication.

Judged on natural ability alone Joe would have earned the ultimate put-down, 'He couldn't kick snow off a rope'. But as a tough-as-teak corner-back, Joe's ferocious commitment meant that he was not alone chosen for the team, he was always captain. His speeches were short affairs.

The most memorable came on the day I won my first medal in the first-year school league final. Its contents in full were:

"If not us – who?

If not now – when?"

But it was the passion that was stamped all over his face, and especially the way he smashed his fist off the bench, that really inspired us. As he whipped us up into a frenzy, Jim was hiding in the dressing-room toilet smoking his customary two fags at a time.

Joe's normal gentle nature off the field was the opposite on it, where he was meaner than a wounded grizzly bear. Everybody dreaded marking him because he tackled with such intensity.

After a big game, Jim treated us to a lengthy expose of how he won it for us, as Joe invariably silently limped away.

My most abiding memory of the two brothers goes back to our first training session for the under-16 championship. The sound of thunder cracked the air and rain spilled down onto the stand roof, rattling like applause on metal slats. It was the kind of wind that seemed to peel the flesh off your bones and come back for the marrow.

Our coach, Br Sean, was a traditionalist. His idea of training was to get us to run multiple laps of the pitch. After the first five he introduced an innovation.

He told us that every time he blew his whistle we were to jump high in the air and imagine we were catching the decisive ball in an All-Ireland final. As the rest of us silently cursed, Joe was way ahead, running like a cheetah and soaring like an eagle to catch imaginary balls.

The drill went on until we got level with the dressing room for the third time. Then Jim, way behind the pack, started to zoom towards the dressing room. Br Sean, his face purple with a mixture of cold and annoyance barked at him, "Where are you going lazy-bones?"

Jim coolly replied, "I'm just going in to get my gloves. That ball you want us to catch is shockin slippy!"

All in the game

Some years ago, at the Seattle Special Olympics, nine disabled contestants assembled at the starting line for the 100-yard dash. At the gun, they all took off in haste. Things were going according to plan until one little boy stumbled on the asphalt, fell, and started to cry. The other eight heard the boy cry. They slowed down and looked back. They all turned around and went back, every one of them. One girl with Down's Syndrome bent down and kissed him and said, "This will make it better".

Then all nine linked arms and walked together to the finish line. Everyone in the stadium stood and cheered.

6

More Than Words

Beautiful quotes can make one stop and wonder. This short chapter contains some lesser-known quotes that invite reflection. They may help to remind us that we belong to a community which is not about a pecking-order, power and authority, but about a humble and humorous sharing of how much we have been blessed.

The Meaning of Life

"The meaning of life comes from the meaning we give it."
(Jim Moran S.J.)

The Leap of Faith

"Faith is taking the first step even when you don't see the full staircase."
(Martin Luther King)

The Happiness Index

"The great essentials for happiness in this life are something to do, something to love, and something to hope for."
(Joseph Addison)

Deep Thinking

"We do not think ourselves into new ways of living, we live ourselves into new ways of thinking."
(Richard Rohr)

With God on My Side?

"My great concern is not whether God is on our side, my great concern is to be on God's side."
(Abraham Lincoln)

With Confidence
....

"Go confidently in the direction of your dreams. Live the life you have imagined."
(Henry David Thoreau)

Act
......

"Ní threabhadh tú pairc go brách á chasadh timpeall i do intinn
- You'll never plough a field by turning it over in your mind."

Habit Forming
....

"We first make our habits and then our habits make us."
(John Dryden)

Choose Wisely
....

"It is not our abilities that show us who we are but our choices."
(*Harry Potter and the Chamber of Secrets*)

The Wonder of You
....

"Too much of a good thing can be wonderful."
(Mae West)

Be Not Afraid

Nelson Mandela encouraged people to let their light shine:
Our deepest fear is not that we are inadequate.
Our deepest fear is that we are powerful
beyond measure!
It is our light, not our darkness, that most frightens us.
We ask ourselves: who am I to be brilliant,
talented, fabulous?
Actually, who are you not to so be?

My Team

Henry Ford's dictum was, *"coming together is a beginning, keeping together is progress; working together is success"*. It is amazing what a team can achieve when no one is bothered about who gets the credit. Teamwork divides the tasks and doubles the success.

Together
Everyone
Achieves
More

Unity is Strength

"By union the smallest states thrive
By discord the greatest are destroyed."
(Sallust)

Farewell

"Farewell! thou art too dear for my possessing,
And like enough thou knowst thy estimate.
The Charter of thy worth gives thee releasing;
My bonds in thee are all determinate.
For how do I hold thee but by thy granting,
And for that riches where is my deserving?
The cause of this fair gift in me is wanting,
And so my patent back again is swerving.
Thy self thou gav'st, thy own worth then not knowing,
Or me, to whom thou gav'st it, else mistaking,
So thy great gift, upon misprision growing,
Comes home again, on better judgement making.
Thus have I had thee as a dream doth flatter:
In sleep a king, but waking no such matter."
(William Shakespeare, *Sonnet 87*)

Fingerlicking Good

"We dipped our fingers in the pockets of God."
(Patrick Kavanagh)

Unconditional

"A friend is somebody who knows you and loves you all
the same."
(Elbert Hubbard)

Salvation

"No one is saved and no one is totally lost."
(Maurice Merleau-Ponty)

Achievement

"Become who you are meant to be."
(Aragorn in *Lord of the Rings*)

Love is All Around

*"All, everything that I understand, I only understand
because I love."*
(Leo Tolstoy)

Giving and Getting

*"When we give cheerfully and accept gratefully, everyone
is blessed."*
(Maya Angelou)

Act Justly

"By doing just acts we come to be just."
(Aristotle)

Sieze the Day
....

*"Look, if you had one shot, or one opportunity to seize
every thing you've ever wanted, one moment, would you
capture it or just let it slip?"*
(Eminem, *Lose Yourself*)

Erosion
....

*"Some guys they just give up living
And start dying little by little, piece by piece."*
(Bruce Springsteen, *Darkness*)

Sleep Well
....

*"Out onto an open road you ride until the day
You learn to sleep at night with the price you pay."*
(Bruce Sprinsteen, *The River*)

Heartfelt
....

*"My words fly up, my thoughts remain below. Words with-
out thoughts never to Heaven go."*
(*Hamlet*, Act 3, Scene 3)

Reality

....

"Humankind cannot bear too much reality."
(T.S. Eliot)

Fame

....

"Fame is a food that dead men eat,
I have no stomach for such meat."
(Henry Austin Dobson, 'Fame Is a Food That Dead Men Eat')

Good Samaritans

....

"On the one hand, we are called to play the Good Samar-
itan on life's roadside, but that will be only an initial act.
One day we must come to see that the whole Jericho road
must be transformed so that men and women will not be
constantly beaten and robbed as they make their journey
on life's highway."
(Martin Luther King)

Win Well

....

"Every time you win, it diminishes the fear a little bit more.
You can never really cancel the fear of losing; you keep
challenging it."
(Arthur Ashe)

Love Heals

....

"Love seeketh not itself to please,
Not for itself any care,
But for another gives its ease,
And builds a Heaven in Hell's despair."
(William Blake, *The Clod and the Pebble*)

True Forgiveness

....

"That cannot be, since I am still possessed
Of those effects for I did the murder:
My crown, mine own ambition, and my queen.
May one be pardoned and retain th' offense?"
(*Hamlet*, Act 3, Scene 3)

Love Deeply

....

"Let me not to the marriage of true minds
Admit impediments. Love is not love
Which alters when it alteration finds ..."
(William Shakespeare, *Sonnet 116*)

One Act of Kindness Can Transform a Life

....

"That light we see is burning in my hall.
How far that little candle throws his beams!
So shines a good deed in a naughty world."
(*The Merchant of Venice* Act 5, Scene 1).

The Ending of Things

"This thou perceiv'st, which makes thy love more strong,
To love that well, which thou must leave ere long."
(William Shakespeare, *Sonnet 73*)

Watch Your Mouth

"The slanderous tongue kills three: the slandered, the slanderer and he who listens to slander."
(The Talmud)

Leadership

"A leader is a man who has the ability to get other people to do what they don't want to do and like it."
(Harry Truman)

Success

"Those who fail to plan, plan to fail.
Luck is infatuated with the efficient."
(Persian Proverb)

Chancy

"Chance favours the prepared mind."
(Louis Pasteur)

Homeward Bound

....

"Home is where we start from."
(T.S. Eliot, *East Coker*)

Preparation

....

"Proper preparation prevents poor performances."
(US Marines)

Planning

....

"Plan your work and work your plan."
(US Army)

Good Luck

....

*"Luck is what happens when preparation meets
opportunity."*
(Darrel Royal, football coach)

If It Be Your Will

....

*"The will to win is not nearly as important as the will to
prepare to win."*
(Bobby Knight, basketball coach)

True Love Ways

....

"We must love one another or die."
(W.H. Auden, *September 1, 1939*)

One-liners

....

1
First I will be prepared, then my chance will come.

2
Timid people rule is that okay?

3
Avoid hangovers. Stay drunk.

4
Little Bo Beep did it for the insurance.

5
A dope peddlar is a sleepy cyclist.

6
History is a thing of the past.

7
Work is the curse of the drinking man.

8
Drive carefully. 90% of people are caused by accidents.

9
42% of people know that all statistics are made up by Homer Simpson.

Testament

....

"The degree of civilization in a society can be judged by entering its prisons."
(Fydor Dostoevsky)

Swan Song

....

"Few men of action have been able to make a graceful exit at the appropriate time."
(Malcolm Muggeridge)

Home, Sweet Home

....

"A house is built of logs and stone,
Of piles and post and piers:
A home is built of loving deeds,
That stand a thousand years."
(Victor Hugo)

Soul-searching

....

"Come, O beautiful soul!
Know, now, that your desire beloved lives hidden within your heart."
(St John of the Cross)

Friendship

"One's sorrow is nothing, but the sorrow one has caused to others makes bitter the bread in the mouth."
(Paul Claudel)

A Friend in Need

"All sufferers have one refuge, a good friend, to whom they can lay bare their griefs and know they will not smile."
(Menander)

I'll Be There for You

"A friend is the one who comes in when the whole world has gone out."
(Spanish Proverb)

Honours Uneven

"It is in the character of very few to honour without envy a friend who has prospered."
(Aeschylus)

Stormy Waters

"After every shipwreck there is enough wood to build a raft."
(Jim Moran S.J.)

Gentleness
....

"Nothing is so strong as gentleness; nothing so gentle as real strength."
(St Francis de Sales)

Heart-warming
....

"Friendship is a word the very sight of which in print makes the heart warm."
(Augustine Birrell)

Goodness
....

"I realised I could not create a new social order in the world without creating a new world order in myself."
(Angelo Pasetto, Communist leader)

In Giving We Receive
....

"We make a living by what we get, but we make a life by what we give."
(Winston Churchill)

A Good Life
....

"Live so that the preacher can tell the truth at your funeral."
(K. Beckstrom)

Gratitude

"The chief idea of my life was that of taking things with gratitude, not for granted."
(G.K. Chesterton)

Don't Worry Be Happy

"We would not worry so much about what people thought of us if we knew how seldom they did."
(Ann Landers)

Challenging Conventional Wisdom

"Do not do unto others as you would have them do unto you - their tastes may not be the same."
(George Bernard Shaw)

The Truth Shall Set You Free

"Truth never damages a cause that is just."
(Mahatma Gandhi)

When Silence is Not Golden

"The cruellest lies are told in silence."
(R.L. Stevenson)

What is the Name of the Game?

"Truth is the cry of all, but the game of few."
(George Berkeley)

Restraint

"Virtue debases itself in justifying itself."
(Voltaire)

The Real Deal

"True happiness comes from the joy of deeds well done, the zest of creating things new."
(Saint-Exupéry)

Nothing but the Truth

"Truth never damages a cause that is just."
(Mahatma Gandhi)

Radiate

"Those who bring sunshine to the lives of others, cannot keep it from themselves."
(Sir James Barrie)

Acceptance

....

"Let us act on what we have, since we have not what we wish for."

(John Henry Newman)

Small is Beautiful

....

"Better a bowl of vegetables where love abides than prime beef garnished with hatred."

(Proverbs 15:17)

Keep the Peace

....

"There is no way to peace - peace is the way."

(Mahatma Gandhi)

Legacy

....

"The best portion of a good man's life: his little nameless, unremembered acts of kindness and love."

(William Wordsworth)

That Loving Feeling

....

"If you love, you will suffer, and if you do not love, you do not know the meaning of a Christian life."

(Agatha Christie)

Empathy

"There are many things that can only be seen through eyes that have cried."
(Oscar Romero)

No Frontiers

"You cannot shake hands with a closed fist."
(Indira Gandhi)

Love Changes Everything

"We come to love not by finding a perfect person, but by learning to see an imperfect person perfectly."
(Sam Keen)

The Windows of Wonder

"Everyone's eyes ought to be windows, but in too many cases they are shutters instead."
(Paul Bailey)

Wellbeing

"And all shall be well, and all shall be well and all manner of things shall be well."
(Julian of Norwich)

About Time

....

"Patience achieves everything."
(Teresa of Avila)

A Rare Breed

....

"Only one person in a thousand is a bore - and they are interesting because they are one in a thousand."
(Sir Harold Nicolson)

Not Killing With Kindness

....

"My religion is very simple - my religion is kindness."
(Dalai Lama)

Aspirational

....

"Aspire not to have more but to be more."
(Oscar Romero)

Destiny's Child

....

"I am the captain of my fate. I am the master of my soul."
(William Ernest Henley)

A Noble Aspiration
....

*"Integrity is more than a charming sentiment to which we
feel we should aspire. It is the only reliable and responsible
connection between ourselves and the world around us."*
(David Puttman)

It's Up to You
....

*"The way you look at things is the most powerful force in
shaping your life."*
(John O'Donohue)

Added Value
....

*"One must not always think so much about what one
should do, but rather what one should be. Our works do not
ennoble us; but we must ennoble our works."*
(Mister Eckhart)

Don't Look Back in Anger
....

*"Finish each day and be done with it. Tomorrow is a new
day. You shall begin it serenely and with too high a spirit
to be encumbered with your old nonsense."*
(Ralph Waldo Emerson)

Because You're Worth It

"Our job is to love others without stopping to inquire whether or not they are worthy."
(Thomas Merton)

Beauty

"See deep enough and you see musically; the heart of nature is everywhere music if you can only reach it."
(Thomas Carlyle)

All Things Bright and Beautiful

"When you reach the heart of life you shall find beauty in all things, even in the eyes that are blind to beauty."
(Kahil Gibran)

Happy Days

"The supreme happiness in life is the conviction that we are loved."
(Victor Hugo)

With Humility

"It takes heroic humility to be yourself."
(Thomas Merton)

Practice Makes Perfect

....

*"An ounce of practice is worth more than
two tons of preaching."*
(Mahatma Gandhi)

Life Lessons

....

*"Life, we've been long together.
Through pleasant and through cloudy weather:
'Tis hard to part when friends are dear
Perhaps 'twill cost a sigh, a tear.
So steal away, give little warning.
Choose your own time."*
(Anna Barbauld)

Mutifaceted

....

*"Blessed is He who has appeared to our human race under
so many metaphors."*
(St Ephrem)

Crossing the Channel

....

*"Life is mostly froth and bubble,
Two things stand like stone.
Kindness in another's trouble,
Courage in one's own."*
(Anon)

New Beginnings

"Every beginning is a promise."
(Brendan Kennelly)

All That Matters

"Nothing matters but the quality of the affection - in the end - that has carved the trace in the mind."
(Ezra Pound)

Travel Safely

"When setting out on a journey, never seek advice from those who have never left home."
(Rumi)

Dreamboat

*"Life is a dream
Tis waking that kills us
He who robs us of our dream robs us of our life."*
(Virginia Wolf)

Faithful Creativity

"To be faithful, to be creative, we need to be able to change."
(Pope Francis)

Grace is in the Air

....

"I do not at all understand the mystery of grace
only that it meets us where we are but does not leave us
where it found us."
(Anne Lamott)

In Hard Times

....

"Had I but one day of life remaining,
Then should I see this generous world I love,
The dawn, the noon, the glorious colour staining
The western sky, the stars serene above
With clearer eye than ever I employ.

"I should be much more eager to forgive
And sympathise, and help and love and pray,
Before the numbered hours had hurried past.
And that is what they must mean when they say
Live every day as if it were the last."
(Anon)

Surprising

....

"I would love to live like a river flows, carried by the sur-
prise of its own unfolding."
(John O'Donohoe)

Building Bridges

....

"Walls solve nothing. We must build bridges."
(Pope Francis)

Disagreements

....

"I like it when someone tells me, 'I don't agree.' This is a true collaborator."
(Pope Francis)

The Long Finger

....

Cork's most famous son, Jack Lynch, also had a way with words. He once made a bold policy statement: "I would not like to leave the repeal of the contraception laws on the long finger."

An Unusual Suggestion

....

Jackie Healy-Rae put his foot in it at a time the tourist industry in Kerry was going through a major slump and Killarney in particular was getting an awful drubbing. To lift the gloom someone suggested that they put gondolas on the lakes of Killarney like they have in Venice. Jackie's retort was: "Who's going to feed the gondolas?"

The Cork Examiner
....

A certain Cork County Councillor made it on to *What it says in Parliament* on BBC radio for two weeks in a row - which was unique at the time. His first quotation came at a meeting of the West Cork Roads Committee when he was asked: "Who shall be chairman?"
He replied, "The chair should rotovate."
The following week at the West Cork Graves Committee he was asked: "How deep should the graves be?"
He replied, "Deep graves are a death trap."

7

And So This is Christmas

As a boy Christmas was always the high point of the year for me - particularly 'Big Saturday', when we all went into town 'to bring home the Christmas' and my sisters and I went to Santa Claus. One year in particular stands out. Armed with a shining two-shilling piece, a gift from my grandfather, the requisite fee for the honour of receiving Santa, I took my place in the queue in a state of high excitement. I was very surprised to see a nun with three small children of the local Travelling family who lived in a big tent by the side of the road. Every time I passed that excuse for a dwelling on my bike I was chilled by the constant chorus of children coughing.

A few months earlier, a family of Travellers had come to live a mile and a half away and been shunned by some of the local community. They were refused entry to some local pubs and shops. At Sunday Mass they sat together on the back seat of the church. None of the 'upright' pillars of the community would sit on the same seat as them. A few of the more superior parishioners decided to go to Mass in the neighbouring parish.

I was going to ask Santa for a pair of boots and a football. However, my plans were modified when I got my first lesson in social awareness, hearing Santa's conversation with the youngest of the Travelling children who was just ahead of me in the queue.

"Now little boy, what will I bring you for Christmas?"

"Please sir, would ya bring me a nice dry blanket to keep me warm on the cauld nights?"

How could I possibly ask for two presents after that? I just asked for a football and did not complain when I discovered that I had got poor value for my two shillings when Santa handed me a cheap-looking colouring book. I think about that incident every time I hear Christy Moore's song *Go Move Shift*, which parallels the original nativity story with the treatment of Travellers.

Christmas is the most wonderful time of the year. It's a thrilling time for giving and for getting, a time for forgiving and for forgetting.

The stories in this chapter celebrate the unique magic that is Christmas. I hope they will provide a smile or two.

The Christmas Gift

Sarah loved her father very much.

He had always done his best for her after his wife died when she gave birth to Sarah eight Christmases ago. He had a head of golden hair, shot through with noble streaks of grey, a fine beard and an imposing physique. He was a solid, dependable character with an ancient but well-maintained leather jacket. He was still a handsome man, with bright brown eyes and fair hair, who continued to win admiring glances from women. Whenever he was asked if he would marry again because Sarah needed a mother, he would shake his head and say, "When you truly love someone you love them forever." Death ends a life but not a relationship. She was always there in his thoughts.

That morning he was not sure how long he had been asleep before he was jolted awake. It was still dark, but he sensed dawn was not far off. He walked outside and watched the town come to life as workers emerged yawning and scratching for a day of honest – or dishonest – toil. Cars of all shapes and sizes flew by. It was hectic and noisy, and over it all came the sound of the bells from St John's Church. So keen was he to move on that he walked too fast, and almost fell when he skidded in the mud. There was a gale of laughter from those watching – louder and longer than was really warranted.

Things were tough for Sarah's dad because there was not much work in the clothes factory now and he could only get work two or three days every week. The owner considered himself to be a superior individual. In his early forties he was smug, conceited and pompous, hailing from a wealthy family. He had a deep, gravelly voice, which dripped hostility. His clothes were the best money could buy, his hair was brushed, and his beard had been fluffed out to impressive proportions. A series of unwise investments and poor financial decisions meant that the factory had been teetering on the brink of fiscal ruin for years.

As a result Sarah's father did not have much money for food and there was going to be no money this year for Christmas presents. He had done his best, but worry was taking its toll, draining even his ebullient spirits.

Sarah had got a tiny tree from her neighbour Deirdre. It was covered in silver tinsel and a few small blue and red ornaments. Sarah had only a little bit of money, which her uncle John had sent her for her birthday last year. She had been saving it all year because she told her father she wanted it for a special occasion, her cherubic face the picture of bemused innocence, although mischief sparkled in her eyes. He smiled when she told him that, winning himself a conspiratorial grin.

On Christmas Eve she went to the local shop, with its windows nearly smothered in poinsettias, and spent all her money on lovely Christmas wrapping paper, with the kind of airy insouciance that suggested she set scant store by financial concerns. Already the traffic was thinning out, everyone trying to get off early, closing shops, going home.

Her father walked home that evening with his coat collar turned up against the icy wind, and a tweed cap pulled over his forehead. A familiar uneasiness settled in his stomach, and he found his hands were shaking, although whether it was as a result of the cold of the star-light night or from anticipating the disappointment he would cause his cherished daughter on Christmas Day, he could not say. By the time he reached his house the human swarm was beginning to thin out. He had not paid any attention to the flow of humanity passing by in front of him. He was normally very gentle and kind but he was very cross that day because he had hardly any money left, and their Christmas dinner was only going to be brown bread and chicken soup. He got very angry when he saw that Sarah had spent all her money on wrapping paper. He started to shout at her but stopped when he saw that he had scared her and she was crying.

Then he said, his voice full of quiet reason: "I'm sorry, Sarah love. I should not have shouted at you. It is your money and you should be able to do what you like with it. Please forgive me, my darling, and let's have a happy Christmas together. Is that okay with you?"

Sarah agreed and quickly dried away all her tears. The ticking of the grandfather clock next to the fireplace pounded fiercely in her head. Her father felt shut out from the Christmas spirit in which the usual standards and words apply.

The next morning Sarah's dad woke up early because light was just beginning to edge past the window shades, suggesting the first hint of morning.

He had gone to bed early and slept like a log, so he rose refreshed and alert. He set about washing and shaving, full of vigour and high spirits, the black thoughts of the previous night forgotten. For now, at least.

He got up purposefully to build a blazing fire, in a manic attempt to stave off the unbearable sadness of last Christmas. Outside, the snow across the park was a vast cascade of white unharmed by footsteps of any kind. A string of lonely Christmas lights on the mantle waited impatiently for an appreciative audience. He was surprised to see that at the door was a box wrapped up in the beautiful wrapping paper that Sarah had bought the day before. He felt bad because he had no money to buy any presents for the daughter he loved so much, but he decided to open the present as he smothered a smile.

It was the one thing he did not expect.

The box was completely empty.

He searched through every inch of it to see if he could find anything, but he could not see anything no matter how hard he searched.

He went down to the cold kitchen where Sarah was preparing the fire, so he clapped her on the back with genuine affection. She was dressed in jeans, a heavy black sweater and boots, looking every inch the woman of the house. Her heels clicked rhythmically on the floor. Her hair was tied back, revealing a small mole near her temple. She looked at him with excitement and asked, "Did you like my Christmas gift Daddy?"

"It was different," said her Dad. "I never got an empty box before."

"That box was not empty Daddy. I filled it with a hundred of my best kisses. This is my box of love."

A big smile came over her father's lips. Sarah ran across the room and hugged him. Her breath warmed his cold neck, sending pockets of energy, of strength, to all corners of his body. He squeezed back gently at first and then he took his daughter up in his arms and hugged her tightly as he said, "Things you know come back to you as if they knew the way. There is no gift I wanted more nor no gift more special in all the land."

A Riverdance Christmas

It had been a tough year for Katy Dobey. That summer her father had died suddenly. At Halloween her mother decided to do something to cheer her up. Mrs Dobey decided that Katy would start dancing classes the following Saturday, and she introduced her daughter to the dancing teacher, who was a tall woman, with dark eyes and smooth brown hair that poked out from under her wimple.

At first Katy was not too pleased with this news, but once she started dancing that first day a new love was born. She was a natural and had never been as happy as she was on the dance floor, especially when she got the chance to perform Riverdance.

After a few weeks the dance teacher took Katy's mother aside and said that she would like to enter her in the talent show in the local town on Christmas morning. The competition was the highlight of the year in the county. Everybody dreamed of winning the massive cup and getting their photo on the front page of the local newspaper. The only problem was that Katy would need a new Riverdance costume. Money was tight on their small farm in the West of Ireland, but Mrs Dobey was determined that she would find the money somehow. That night she called to see the manager of the furniture factory that her husband had worked in. He readily agreed to Mrs Dobey's request for a part-time job cleaning the factory floor.

Later that week Katy went with her mother to meet Mrs Mighty, the dressmaker. A thick, drenching drizzle fell as they walked. As they crossed the bridge they had their first glimpse of the church. It was unusually large and had been the subject of a recent renovation, as parts of it were still swathed in scaffolding. The windows high above allowed light to flood in, even on dull days.

Mrs Mighty had the reputation of being the best dressmaker in all of Ireland, but she was a sad and bitter old woman. She was a tall, thin lady though she was stooped like the man Katy had seen in the film *The Hunchback of Notre Dame*. Although she was widely respected for her special talent she was not a little feared because of her fierce temper and her rough manner with people. Twenty years previously, on Christmas Eve, Mrs Mighty's husband and three children had been killed by a drunk driver.

The weeks coming up to Christmas were the loneliest time of the year for her. In the town, she belonged to a club of one: she was the only woman who hated Christmas.

She felt like a stone had crushed her heart. Occasionally she showed flashes of tenderness, but by and large she was too damaged to love anyone from that day on. The nickname her neighbours gave her was 'the dragon' though no one would dare call her that to her face.

"What do you want?" demanded Mrs Mighty as soon as Katy came in the door. She had a voice like a growling dog and Katy was terrified of her straight away, though she noticed that the dressmaker was pale and that there was a moistness around her eyes that suggested tears. She was of indeterminate age, and wore a fine blue dress.

"I . . . we would very much like if you would make a Riverdance costume for Katy here," answered Mrs Dobey.

"When would you want it for?", snapped Mrs Mighty.

"By Christmas Eve please," said Katy sweetly.

"Christmas Eve," shouted Mrs Mighty angrily. "That's only five weeks away. Do you have any idea how busy I am? I'll have it ready for Christmas Eve but it'll be Christmas next year." Her words were full of menace.

Katy nearly jumped out of her skin with fear. Her face was ashen and she fought in vain to hold back the tears. Katy had one of the loveliest faces Mrs Mighty had ever seen, not just for its even features, clear skin and blue eyes, but for its expression of astonishing sweetness.

A heavy, awkward silence settled on the room. Mrs Dobey took Katy by the hand and was about to walk out when Mrs Mighty unexpectedly said, "Wait a second. I'm not promising anything, mind, but maybe I might be able to do something. Little girl, let me have a quick look at you again. Oh, stop crying! Okay call back to me Tuesday evening at seven and we'll see."

Mrs Dobey said, "Thanks very much Mrs Mighty."

Drat it. Why didn't I just send them packing especially as I hate Christmas? thought Mrs Mighty to herself as soon as the door was closed. All the same there was something about that little girl.

She went into the kitchen, picked up an old milk carton and started scribbling furiously on it. In spite of herself, a small smile crept over her face when she saw the finished design for the Riverdance costume.

That Tuesday evening Katy didn't want to go back to Mrs Mighty, she was so scared of her, but her mother made her. The dressmaker had her measuring tape ready when they called. The only words she said to them were "Come in" and when she finished expertly measuring Katy she said, "Little Miss, Madam, I want to see you here every Saturday 'til Christmas Eve."

Each Saturday Katy's eyes grew wider as she saw the costume taking shape and getting ever more beautiful. Although they never said much to each other, she began to like Mrs Mighty, and for her part, the dressmaker secretly started to look forward to Katy's visits because she was such a sweet girl.

At last Christmas Eve came and it was finally time to collect the costume. "I've never seen anything so lovely. It must be the eighth wonder of the world!" said Mrs Dobey with awe in her voice. Indeed, nobody had ever seen such a stunning costume.

After Mrs Dobey paid the dressmaker her fee, Katy handed her a big bag. "Happy Christmas Mrs Mighty and thanks for all your hard work. This gift isn't much. I wish I could have got you more," she said.

The old woman opened the bag and pulled out a pair of red gloves and a green cap with Mrs Mighty embroidered on it, which Katy had knitted herself, as well as a Christmas card. Mrs Mighty looked shocked. "It's been ten years since anyone sent me a Christmas card and much longer since anyone gave me a present. Thank you so much Katy. I can't find the words to tell just how much this means to me."

Katy wasn't really sure whether Mrs Mighty was happy or sad, but something deep inside herself told her to lean forward and give the old woman a kiss. This only made Mrs Mighty's tears come all the quicker. By now poor Katy was really confused. She gathered up her new dancing costume and quickly made her farewell.

On Christmas morning Katy woke early, long before the first faint flickers of light lit up the specks of frost on the hard ground. After a light breakfast it was time to head into the town hall. Katy felt a peculiar mixture of anxiety and anticipation. The other contestants all looked so sophisticated, pretty and intelligent. She was third last to compete. The butterflies were going mad in her stomach as she stepped onto the stage. She had never seen so many people. Every seat was taken and there seemed to be hundreds of people standing at the back. Then her music tape was turned on. Katy's Riverdance was exuberant, extravagant, unpredictable; like a toboggan run: dangerous and exhilarating. She finished with a yelp of unrestrained joy. The audience went wild, and her heart was beating like the sails of a mill on a gale.

Twenty minutes later the Master of Ceremonies stood up to give the results. He was small, with a wispy beard that gave him the appearance of a youth unable to produce the more luxurious whiskers of an older man. Only the lines of worry and tiredness around his mouth and eyes suggested that he was loaded with the considerable responsibility of running the biggest factory in the town. Every head turned towards him, so he drew himself up to his full height, and looked around with an imperious gaze.

There were a sharp gasp of astonishment from Katy, which quickly gave way to sheer happiness as the result was announced and she was declared the winner.

After the cup was presented, Katy left the stage and went to greet her mother, who was with another woman. At first Katy did not recognise her, but as she got closer she could not believe her eyes when she realised it was Mrs Mighty. She was wearing beautiful clothes and make-up and had put dark tints in her hair. She looked at least 20 years younger as she removed her beautiful hat with an elegant flourish, her bearing regal.

"Is that really you Mrs Mighty?" asked Katy. "You look so . . You're so pretty now."

Mrs Mighty laughed heartily before saying, "Thanks for the compliment Katy... I think! For too long I have lived in the past with all my sadness and anger. You have reminded me that the greatest Christmas gift of all is the present. From now on I will live each precious day as if it was my last. For the first time since my husband died, I've had a happy Christmas. I've discovered again that this is a time of mystery, magic, hope and above all, innocence. It's all thanks to you Katy. I'm so grateful."

Love Hurts

....

One day the vicar's car broke down on the way to a wedding ceremony and he was an hour late on arrival. The wedding party was beginning to panic when he arrived, their face taut with worry and the vicar was so embarrassed seeing the distress in everybody's expressions he never forgot the incident. The groom was a teacher. His name was Andrew and he was a tall, fair, amiable and placid fellow, seldom roused to anger, even when he had the most cheeky and disruptive pupils in his care like Ciaran, who was short, dark and sly, and of course the red-haired Peadar, who was one of the laziest lads he had ever encountered.

The wedding took place on a glorious summer afternoon, with fluffy white clouds flecking an impossibly blue sky, trees whispering softly in a gentle breeze, and the lazy sound of bees humming among the hedgegrows. Cows lowed contentedly in the distance, and the air was rich with the scent of ripe corn and scythed grass.

There had been a fierce heatwave earlier that year, followed by torrential rains that had devastated farmland all over the country. Fortune had smiled on this area, though: its crops had survived the treacherous weather, and the harvest was expected to be excellent. It was already evident that the local farmers would not go short of bread that winter, and the fat sheep and cattle dotting the surrounding hills indicated they would not be short of meat, either.

But the father of the bride saw none of this plenty; his mind was on another matter entirely. His only daughter was a slim, elegant woman who took considerable pride in her appearance. She loved clothes, and spent a lot of her father's money ensuring she was never less than perfectly attired, from her always fashionable hat to her stylish designer brand shoes. Her weakness for finery exasperated her father, who was always reminding her that while he was not a poor farmer, he was not exactly wealthy, either, and that he had a duty to her seven brothers to use the profits from the family farm more wisely than frittering them away on extravagancies. His face went white with anger when he thought of all the money his daughter had cost him. The one bright note on his horizon was that from now on Andrew would have to foot his daughter's bills. Her trusting husband would get an introduction into 'for richer or poor poorer' much sooner than he ever could have envisaged.

Twenty years later, the vicar met Andrew at a Christmas function in a local hotel for a fundraiser for the St Vincent de Paul. It was cold, even for the festive time of the year, and as he got out of his car the vicar could see his breath pluming in front of him as he sprinted out of the carpark towards the warmth of the hotel. There was a rainy snow in the air, too, spiteful little droplets carried in a bitter wind that stung where they hit. He had forgotten his watch so he glanced up at the sky, trying to guage the hour. Other than the disturbance caused by the howls of a dog, the town was virtually silent, and the velvety blackness indicated that he was very late again and it was near the darkest part of the night, perhaps close to midnight.

As soon as he got inside the door after seeing an elderly woman staggering in, puffing like a pair of bellows, he greeted the organiser and mumbled, "I am sorry for being late", in the automatic way that suggested these were words uttered on far too regular a basis.

The vicar was tired because he had spent the afternoon in the church yard giving it its annual Christmas tidy-up, even though it had been another cold, gloomy day, with clouds thick and heavy overhead. It had been windy too, and autumn leaves swirled around until they made soggy piles in corners. He had breathed in deeply, relishing the clean scent of damp vegetation. The only fly in the ointment was when he whipped around in alarm as he heard a sound close behind him, but it was only the parish secretary. This was a man who prided himself on his stealth, and was always sneaking up on people with the clear intention of making them jump out of their skin.

The town's forefathers had chosen an idyllic spot for their community. It was just south-west of the castle, on what was effectively an island with two arms of the river sweeping around it. It boasted a range of impressive new and old buildings, along with gardens and an orchard, although it was the church that most caught the eye. This was a wonderful creation of soft grey stone, with tiers of large windows to let in the light. Stone seats were provided for restful reposes in the adjacent park during summer, while a tinkling fountain offered an attractive centrepiece.

The cool air had smelled of wet soil and coming spring blossom, and was damp from a recent shower. A black-bird trilled a final song from the roof of the church, clear and sweet, while a neighbour sang lustily in her kitchen. Other than that, the evening was still, and the vicar was aware of a growing sense of peace. He breathed in deeply, enjoying the sweet scents of the fading day.

The yard was full of his predecessors' tombs, and was a dark, silent, intimate place. Inside the church an elderly nun had been praying, although her nodding head and bowed shoulders suggested that her sleepless night was beginning to catch up with her. She turned at the sound of footsteps and heaved herself to her feet, yawning hugely as she did so.

At the back of the church there had been a man so still and poised that he might have been a statute, but then he sneezed, and spoiled his attitude of elegant piety by wiping his nose on his overcoat. He sneezed again, sniffed loudly, and this time it was his sleeve that cleaned his running nose.

The rain had passed, and the day had turned pretty, with fluffy white clouds dotting a bright blue sky and a warm sun drawing steam from the wet ground. The appetising scent of frying eggs wafted from within a wel-coming house. The work in the yard had been exhausting but the vicar would have gladly swapped it for what he was facing at the function.

He could not help but overhear snippets of conver-sation as he wove though the tables. As he slumped gratefully into a chair in the corner of the reception room in the hotel and secretly wished he was at home in front of the fire watching *Match of the Day,* his sharp expression softened as he saw Andrew for the first time in years. He beckoned the teacher over and shook his hand and smiled as he said: "I'm so sorry about that horrible fright I gave you on your wedding day."

"So am I," said the man, so venomously that the vicar was repelled by the malice that blazed from his face. In truth Andrew did not look well. His face was pale, and his eyes were watery. He smiled, although it was not a pleasant expression. Andrew set heavily on a nearby chair, and the vicar saw the colour drain from his face. He appeared to be on the verge of exhaustion as he said with real feeling. "I've still got her!"

Ugly Betty

Sr Mary was exhausted.

Every Christmas Eve she organised a big party for the children in the local orphanage. It was always the highlight of the year for them. Every evening since the first of December she had been busy baking all kinds of the most delicious cakes and buns for the feast at the finish.

She also arranged for the local shops to donate toys and presents so that each child could get a special gift, and then she wrapped them in her own dazzling display of Christmas decorating paper.

Every child's favourite part of the day at the party was when Sr Mary told a story. This year she had told the one about Ugly Betty, the queen of Ulster in days gone by. Betty had the ears of the horse, which made her feel angry and ashamed. Since she was not prepared to be laughed at by allowing her ears to be seen, she wore her hair very long, and the hairdresser visited the palace only once a year at Christmas. It was a different hairdresser every year, because the poor hairdresser was put into prison forever so that she could never tell anyone about the queen's big ears.

One Christmas the queen, who had a good heart, decided to let the hairdresser go free as long as she promised never to tell anyone her secret. The poor hairdresser, Martha, was so afraid of telling anyone Ugly Betty's secret that she went and asked her grandmother, who was famous far and wide for her wisdom, how she would keep her secret. So her grandmother advised Martha to go to a forest and tell a tree her secret. Martha did as she was told and immediately she felt better.

The tree was a willow tree and a few weeks later it was cut down to make a new harp for the queen's orchestra. On Christmas Eve the whole kingdom of Ulster gathered for the Christmas concert, but when the music started the audience heard the sounds coming from the new harp saying:

"The Queen has horse's ears."

There was stunned silence.

Then the harp started to play again and this time the words that came from it were:

"But do not mind her ears
Because she has a good heart
And that is all that matters."

And everyone got on to their feet and clapped and cheered for the queen's good heart. From that Christmas on the queen never worried about her ears again, and all her hairdressers were released from prison. Soon Ulster became known as the kingdom of kindness.

After the party Sr Mary was sitting by the window in the huge hall on the ground floor, with two chambers for sleeping above it, as she opened a letter from home and found a £20 note inside as her Christmas gift from her family in Kerry.

Sr Mary was a big believer in knowing the true meaning of Christmas. While reading the letter she noticed a poor beggar sitting in the rain outside. She jumped out of her seat and wrapped the £20 note in a piece of paper which carried a simple message: "Have courage. Sister Mary." She threw it out the window and the beggar accepted it gleefully.

On St Stephen's Day Sr Paula, the cross-looking Mother Superior, approached Sr Mary in the study and with a raised eyebrow and a strong sense of disapproval and told her that 'a shabby man' was at the door, who was insisting on seeing her. Her face was black with anger as she left the room, and her irate muttering remained audible even as she walked purposefully down the corridor. Dark clouds massed over the leafy darkness of the convent, promising an early dusk and rain before morning.

A puzzled Sr Mary found the beggar waiting. He handed her £200 without a word.

"What's this?" she asked.

"Have Courage came in at ten to one in the 1.30 at Leopardstown."

Silence is Golden

Once a great preacher was coming to visit a remote village in the mountains for the Christmas celebrations, bringing a sudden end to the fascinating spectacle of people hurling insults at each other in the street. So excited were the local villagers that they spent days preparing the questions they were going to put to the holy man. His calm, sober manner and his reluctance to become embroiled in a public squabble with the most trying people had won the admiration of many. It was said that he had more goodness in his little finger than was to be found in the souls of a hundred monks.

When dawn came, it was with a blaze of colour. The sky lightened gradually, then distant clouds were painted grey, orange, pink, and finally gold. The preacher awoke early although there were lines under his eyes that suggested that he had slept badly, but he was still cheerful and patient with everyone. He was never sharp-tongued. Indeed, he had the patience of a saint when dealing with people many would have regarded as unworthy of such courtesy, even when they were remarkable only for their arrogance, self-interest and ambition, although in exceptional circumstances his eyes could turn dangerously cold.

The preacher walked to his destination with a heavy heart, barely acknowledging the greetings of people he knew. He met an old friend mostly recovered from his drunken revelry, but did not feel like lingering to chat.

It was a pretty day, with a crisp scent of late autumn in the air. The trees were red and gold, and showers of leaves drifted across the road each time the wind blew. A pheasant croaked crossly from deep in the woods, and a cow lowed in a nearby meadow. A woman smiled thinly as she demanded the latest gossip. There was ice in her voice. A neighbour gave her a look of such disdain that she felt herself bristle.

The preacher tipped his head back and took a deep breath, savouring the smell of damp leaves and sweet soil.

Instead of speaking, the preacher looked into the eyes of everybody in the group. He gave an empty grin, full of misshapen teeth, and waved. Then he began to softly hum a strange melody. Soon everyone began to hum with him.

After some time the preacher started to sway and dance in solemn, measured steps. His audience did likewise. Gradually the crowd became so immersed in the dance that they forget all their problems and anxieties. Nobody dared to blurt an interruption and people's faces visibly softened towards their enemies, and they laid apologetic arms across each other's shoulders.

An hour later the dance slowed to a dead halt. By that time the crowd were totally relaxed and at peace with themselves. They savoured together the sense of peace and community that the preacher had created. Then the preacher spoke the only words that passed his lips all evening with a careless shrug: "I come to you this Christmas because I had been asked to voice concern for you, my brethren. I hope that I have answered all your questions."

Sick as a Parrot

Simon was the seventh son of a seventh son and had what was known locally as 'the gift'. People came from miles around for him to lay their hands on him in a desperate hope that he would cure them. I had to visit him once myself in his professional capacity when I fell victim to the highly infectious rural disease - ringworm. My arm was invaded by an unsightly and maddeningly itchy scab. Simon placed his hand in a bowl of holy water and made the sign of the cross on it. He rubbed some kind of homemade concoction on my arm. It looked awful and smelt worse, but it took away the itch and stopped me scratching.

He was a small, slight man. In many ways he was a child who had never grown up. He loved a good yarn but was never unduly bothered about trifles like veracity. At heart though, he was a good man. That was why he gave his niece, Sr Rita, a parrot for Christmas.

If Sr Rita had been given her choice, that was not the gift she would have chosen, because a convent was not the ideal home for a bird who talked. Her initial instinct was quickly proved to be correct. The bane of her life was the Reverend Mother who seemed to go out of her way to make Sr Rita's life a misery. After one particularly humiliating chastisement in front of the entire community, when she got back to the sanctuary of her room she shouted out in sheer frustration, "I hope Reverend Mother dies."

She burst into tears because she had never felt so low. Her only consolation was that things could not possibly get any worse.

She was wrong.

From his new home in the corner of his room her parrot exclaimed, "I hope Reverend Mother dies. I hope Reverend Mother dies."

For the next week Sr Rita's nerves were fraught with tension because the parrot would not stop repeating that sentence.

Eventually she could take no more and she went to the only person she could think of to help her, Fr Tom, the local parish priest. He nodded with an expression that exuded kindness and sympathy as he listened to her predicament. At first he frowned his bemusement at the situation. Then he smiled in triumph at the end of her story as he announced without preamble, "I have the perfect solution. I will take your parrot off you and put him alongside my parrot, who is incredibly pious and that will put an end to your problems."

The next day Sr Rita, surging to her feet with a grin of happy anticipation, moved her parrot into the parochial house and the two parrots struck up an immediate rapport and they all lived happily ever after.

Well, they did until the next Christmas morning.

As was her tradition, the Reverend Mother called over to Fr Tom to give him his Christmas present, a large bottle of brandy, after morning Mass.

The parish church had been packed to overflowing and the atmosphere was slightly tense as people jockeyed for the best places. The Reverend Mother's face was pale and waxy. She was clutching her arm almost desperately, but she was more interested in nodding greetings to the people she knew as she came out of the church. She spoke in a voice that had a peculiarly booming quality.

Handel's *Messiah* blasted uplifting tones from the old radio in the parochial house.

As soon as she went into the living room Sr Rita's parrot said "I hope Reverend Mother dies. I hope Reverend Mother dies."

Fr Tom froze.

There was a pregnant pause.

Then the other parrot piped up: "Lord graciously hear us."

When Joseph Met Mary

....

Once upon a time about 2,000 years there was a couple who were very much in love. The man's name was Joseph and his wife was Mary.

They travelled from Nazareth to Bethlehem for the census. It was a difficult journey made all the more challenging because Mary was nine months pregnant and was due to give birth at any moment. When they got to Bethlehem there was no room for them in the inn, so they had to find shelter in a damp, dusty stable. It was not long before Mary fell into a deep sleep. Joseph took the opportunity to slip out into the night air. On the way to the stable he had noticed Bethlehem's only 24-hour shop. It was run by Katy Kindheart who was known as the kindest woman in the kingdom.

"Excuse me Miss. I am very sorry but I have no money," Joseph said.

Katy smiled kindly at him and said, "Don't worry, sir we accept Mastercard, Visa and all major credit cards."

Joseph shook his head sadly and said, "I am afraid the only card I have is my Tesco bonus card." He took it out of his pocket and held it up for her to see.

Katy smiled sweetly at him and said: "That's very nice sir, but I'm afraid it's no good here."

Joseph let out a big sigh and said: "I should have known that. I'm sorry for wasting your time." He turned and walked away dejected.

Katy shouted at him: "Wait. What did you want to ask me?"

Joseph turned around and said, "I don't want to ask anything for myself but my wife is about to give birth to our first baby. We have no food left at all and she hasn't eaten all day and I would love to get six eggs to make her an omlette in the morning."

Katy said gently, "Oh you poor man and your poor wife. Of course take six eggs, here."

Joseph answered, "I couldn't possibly accept something for nothing from anyone, especially a stranger. Please take this ring that my wife gave me for our wedding. I know it is worth very little but it is the only thing I have apart from the clothes on my back."

Katy replied, "I couldn't possibly take your wedding ring. Here take the eggs as a gift."

Joseph said, "Thank you for the kind offer, but I am a proud man and can't possibly take them from you unless you accept the ring."

Katy shrugged her shoulders, "Very well. If you insist. But I insist you take two dozen eggs then and not six."

Joseph said, "That is very kind of you," as he took the eggs and handed Katy the ring.

Katy replied, "Goodnight then. I hope things work out well for you."

Joseph tiptoed softly back to the stable and lay down exhausted. Although he was delighted to have some food for his wife, his heart was heavy because he had given away his prize possession, his wedding ring. Despite all his cares and worries he too fell into a deep sleep. Shortly after Mary woke and saw her husband's exhaustion she decided to go on a mission of her own. She sneaked softly out of the stable and headed for the shop she had passed on the way.

Katy smiled sweetly at her and said, "Good evening Madam. How may I help?"

Mary answered in a tired, sleepy voice, "I'm afraid it's a long story. You see my husband and I have travelled all the way from Bethlehem. We have very little food and my husband hasn't eaten for five days because he has given all his food to me. I would love to be able to cook some scrambled eggs for his breakfast in the morning because he has been so good to me. The problem is I have no money."

Katy nodded in understanding, "I understand. Please take these six eggs with my compliments."

Mary smiled weakly and said: "Thank you for the kind offer. I couldn't possibly accept them, without giving you something in return. My husband gave me this chain to me on the day of our wedding. It is the only thing I own. Please take it, otherwise I can't accept your eggs."

Katy raised her hands in protest, "Really, there is no need for payment."

Mary replied sharply, "I must insist."

Katy smiled softly, "Well, if that's what you want. But I insist on giving you a dozen eggs."

The two women exchanged eggs for the chain. Katy said warmly, "Good luck with your baby."

Mary answered: "Thank you and good night."

Katy Kindheart again shook her head sadly after her customer left.

Mary returned quietly to the stable and within a short time she started moaning.

A few minutes later Mary's boy child was born and they called him Jesus.

An angel appeared from Heaven and announced the birth of the baby with soft, sweet music that could some-how be heard throughout the whole kingdom.

Within minutes, shepherds and their wives came and brought beautiful gifts to the new baby. As things calmed down they were joined by a shy shepherd's daughter with her violin who said, "I would love to offer the Christ child gold and silver but my simple gift is my music. This is all I can give you."

The girl played the sweetest music that Joseph and Mary had ever heard.

It was around then that Katy Kindheart decided to visit the stable. By now it was hard to see her way. It was a dark night, as black as the ace of spades. Not a star was to be seen. It was bitterly cold. Only a purring cat shattered the spell of silence. Katy's breath was coming out like puffs of steam from a kettle. Snowflakes began to fall, timidly at first, then getting very strong as the shyness appeared to wear off them.

A few swirling snowflakes drifted onto her head. Katy guessed her way along the side of the road, and once she stumbled and almost fell into a wet ditch. She plodded up the pathway, through the thickening snow-storm, leaving big, deep footprints in the fresh snow.

Strangely Katy still felt happy, though now the snow was making a white carpet on her hair. The whole sky seemed to be filled with dizzy, dancing snow. The blanket of snow created a light that gave life to hedges and houses, so that night started to look like day.

Even before she got to the door Katy could hear the new baby crying. She saw a few men rushing in before them in a state of great excitement. Some of them were carrying armfuls of nice, clean straw.

Katy walked in and peeped out from behind one of the big men to see Mary holding her new baby, and no woman could have looked happier. A lot of happy visitors were circling the happy couple like a swarm of bees. Outside, children's screams pierced the frosty air. The late-comers frantically scampered up to the door, slipping red-faced into a corner at the back, briefly disturbing the hushed stillness. Men in heavy coats shuffled nervously, whispering about the price of sheep over the talk about the new baby. Women in their best coats held their heads high.

There were a lot of holes in the stable walls, so a chilly wind was blowing through, giving Katy the shivers.

She heard one of the shepherds whispering, "Then it is true. About an hour ago an angel appeared to us as we sat around our campfire. We were tired from looking after our sheep all day and very cold so we had been drinking whiskey to keep us warm. The first thing the angel said was 'Be not afraid.' But we were terrified! Really, I mean it. We were sacred out of our wits! We had never seen an angel before. We thought we must have done something very wrong or that we were in trouble for drinking whiskey.

"We had never looked at an angel nor smelled an angel nor heard an angel's voice. The angel's voice was kind of strange, like nothing we had ever heard before. The smell the angel gave off was so pure it almost hurt our noses. Then the angel said a second time, 'Be not afraid.' And once again we were terrified! The angel went on to say, 'Tonight a child is born who will save the world.' Just when we thought things could get no stranger the angel started singing. Over and over again it sang, 'Glory to God in the highest and peace to all people on earth. Listen now and hear what I have to say. All children will live for ever more because of Christmas Day.' The angel told us that we would never feel really bad again and that there would always be a light in our hearts and that we should go and see this new baby by following a star in the East. That's what we tried to do but the star was high in the sky and once it started snowing we couldn't see it anymore and we got lost. Before I got here we were starting to wonder if we had imagined it all because you never expect you will get a visit from an angel."

Katy had brought two baskets with her, one filled with cakes and delicious food, the other filled with nappies, soaps and towels. Hidden in beneath she also left Joseph's wedding ring and Mary's chain.

She said, "Congratulations Mary. I had no idea you were to be the mother of such a special baby. All of Bethlehem is talking about nothing else. She went on to say, "Congratulations to you Joseph. I have an apartment outside Bethlehem and I insist you stay in it for the next week."

Joseph and Katy gave each other a big hug. Katy turned and said to all the people in the stable, "Our lives are not measured by the number of breaths we take but by the moments that take our breath away - this is such a moment. A ray of hope is flickering across the sky. A child has been born who will turn the world on its head and heal the sick, give sight to the blind, feed the poor and bring the world eternal life. His love will shine a light into every corner of the world. Come now, let us leave these people in peace. I'm going home to play with my cat."

Joseph asked: "Oh what's it called?"

Katy answered with a cheeky grin: "Santa PAWS."

Everybody left the stable to leave the two new parents alone with their baby.

Mary turned to her husband and said, "I don't need an occasion to be romantic for the man I love, but I wanted to say thank you for being there for me through all that is happened. Why did you really fall for me in the first place?"

Joseph said, "You have the one quality that I always look for in a woman?"

Mary asked, "Which is?"

Joseph looked at her shyly. "You were crazy enough to like me."

Mary answered, "Crazy - me? Never. Despite all that has happened, meeting you is the best thing that ever happened to me."

Joseph said: "You say the sweetest things. How can I trump that? Meeting you, meeting you . . ."

Mary butted in and said, "You don't have to make something up. There's no substitute for sincerity."

Joseph said, "You are so gorgeous that every time you walk into the room my heart beats faster. I still remember the stammer that came into my voice the first time I spoke to you. Meeting you has turned my life around. You have made me the happiest man alive."

Mary laughed as she said, "After a slow start you came

with a powerful finish. Thank you kind sir. Thank you Joseph, thanks to you I am the happiest woman in the world."

Joseph, though, had some more compliments to offer: "Mary, you are a Goddess walking among women. Is there anything I could do to make this the perfect night for you?"

Mary looked hopefully at her husband, "I would love you to sing me that old Jewish folk song you sang that night we first met."

Joseph sang a song which told about a man who was constantly amazed by the beauty and wonder of his wife.

Mary said, "Thank you Joseph. That was beautiful."

Joseph answered, "Mary, it is not that you are the love of my life - you are my life.

"Let us leave now for that apartment Katy Kindheart is lending us for the next week."

Joseph took the baby in his arms and left the stable holding Mary's hand.

The weather had taken a turn for the worse overnight. There was a persistent and drenching downpour that looked set to continue for the rest of the day, the sky was a solid, unbroken grey, and everything dripped. There was a spurt of new growth in the hedgerows but their bright colours were dulled by the sullen light.

Sadly it would not be fair to say that Joseph, Mary and Jesus lived happy ever after. However, despite all the setbacks they faced and all the tragedy they experienced, not a single day went by without Mary and Joseph falling ever more deeply in love.

Every Christmas Day Joseph would say the same thing to Mary: "Christmas came to me when my heart found yours."

Unto Us A Child Is Born

Christmas really begins in the Cistercian monastery in Roscrea in Co. Tipperary with the carol service. Crowds gather, young and old, just to savour the beauty and wonder of it all. Some old customs can momentarily transfigure our existence and let the eternal shine through. One such custom is the singing of carols. They strike us as simple ways of expressing those parts of Christianity that ordinary people find most interesting, not the parts that people ought to find most interesting. They are memorable because they are so tangible. They celebrate things that we can touch and see and warm to: a mother and a baby, though curiously not a father, or at least not a real father, a stable, donkeys, shepherds, straw and hay.

Another important part of preparation for the season is the making of the monastery's Christmas cards. These will not be showing old world people in 18th and 19th century clothes walking about snowy landscapes, but rather capture some element of the religious dimension of the season of goodwill.

Here in the monastery, in common with all Irish families before Christmas, a great clean-up begins and every room in the house is turned upside down and inside out as if very special visitors were coming. Everything is dusted, swept, scrubbed, scoured or polished, curtains are washed, and every place looks at its very best by the end.

Of course for the Cistercians, the most important preparation is spiritual and the preparation has gone on throughout Advent. It is a time to connect with the real meaning of Christmas. Favourite Christmas stories are retold, like the story of how Christmas stopped a war when the fierce and bloody first World War came to a halt on the day of Christ's birth in one corner of the western front. The Germans waved and called out speaking in simple French, holding out cigars they asked for English jam in return. *Stille Nacht* and *Silent Night* rang out on different sides. The words were different but the sentiments remained the same. A football was produced and a game of soccer took place. Music and sport, two of the languages which could have united the participants at the tower of Babel. For a moment at least, compassion carried more power than cruelty.

Advent is a time to embrace the compassionate God. As the Dalai Lama pointed out: "If you want others to be happy, practice compassion. If you want to be happy, practice compassion."

Advent is also a time of prayer, helping us to open ourselves to the healing presence of the Lord. In the words of Mahatma Gandhi: "The rose transmits its scent without a movement. I have a definite feeling that if you want us to experience the aroma of Christianity, you must copy the rose. It irresistibly draws people to itself and the scent remains with them. A rose does not preach. It simply spreads its fragrance."

In the past Christmas Eve was the day when some Irish people finished their 4,000 Hail Marys, which they began on the first day of Advent. Inevitably many began the season by faithfully saying their daily quota of 156 Hail Marys, but they let the practice slip in the middle of the month and then in the final few days, they had to bombard the heavens with prayers.

Advent is the season of the head and Christmas is the season of the heart. For the Cistercians, Advent is a time of self-questioning, a time that challenges them to integrate their faith and life in the modern world. Christmas, then, is a reminder of a wonderful message: God has transformed out brokenness by taking it on.

In Roscrea though, there is also a very keen awareness of the pastoral dimension of Christmas. Every year they remember those who are bruised and broken, melancholic or moody. They pray for those who in a peculiar way both look forward to the season of 'good cheer' and dread it, and for those who are impatient for the magic that never comes for them but all the preparations promise. Christmas is above all a time for them to be lonely.

In times of emigration they remember those with families scattered all over the world, England, Australia, America and Canada. Some feel exile, home-sickness, longing and hoped-for returns that would never materialise, and are trapped in a prison of memories. Their pain is the piercing grief of never being able to return to the way things used to be.

They also recall the elderly people who live alone and whose loneliness become more intense and shrill with each passing Christmas - at times ascending to a chilling crescendo. Every year their longing for warmth and affection becomes more desperate. They are other silent victims of a vast and concealed cancer of loneliness. Christmas is little more than a painful reminder of missed chances for lasting happiness.

Traditionally in rural Ireland in dark's dull density, the curtains were stripped off the windows and a single candle was put to burn in each sill until the morning. When the rosary was said, the children were dispatched to an early night in bed, and no dissenting voice was raised. Across the fields, the houses glittered, the light from their candles like jewelled pin-points in the darkness. The back door remained unlocked whatever the weather, so that there was no danger of Mary and Joseph going astray in their search for a resting place. The Cistercians in Roscrea continue in the Irish tradition of monastic hospitality where the marginalised were welcomed. Hospitality was often very much in the tradition of the story of the widow's mite. Although they had very little to offer they gave generously, sharing the view of St Francis of Assisi: "it is in giving that we receive".

The tradition of the 'Ireland of the Welcomes' can be traced back to pre-Christian times. Under the Brehon laws, to refuse hospitality was not simply impolite, it was considered an offence. The arrival of Christianity gave a new impetus to this tradition. In the Judgement Gospel (Matthew 25) hospitality is seen as an integral part of the Christian life: "I was a stranger and you welcomed me". Hospitality was actually institutionalised in the Irish monasteries with each having its own *Teach Aíochta* (House of Hospitality). The monks supplied food, drink and overnight accommodation to all passers-by without seeking any financial donation.

In the Celtic tradition and for the Cistercians in Roscrea, the guest is always Christ and hospitality is offered to the Christ in the other.

Thomas Merton said, "With those for whom there is no room is Jesus." The Cistercians believe that especially at Christmas, with those for whom there is no one to share their rooms is Jesus. The sad reality is that life is difficult for many people. The message of Christmas in Roscrea is that Christ is made flesh not in the unreal beauty of the Christmas card, but in the mess that is our world. For those of us who claim to be Christian, Christ is made flesh in our neighbours.

Oh Happy Day

On Christmas morning the Cistercians wake early, long before the first faint vestiges of light illuminate the speck-lings of frost on the hard ground. Sometimes as they pull back the curtains they are compelled to watch the world take shape despite their haste. The faint horizontal threads of clouds grow a fiercer red against the still grey sky, the streaks intensifying to scarlet and to orange and to gold, until the whole sky is a breath-taking symphony of colour. The stars are like holes in God's carpet which allow the eternal light to shine through.

A hoar frost lay on the fields and the hedgerows were hung with the lace trimmings of what seems to be a thousand spiders' webs. In the distance cattle are huddling under creeping hedges, staring vacantly up at the emerging slate-grey sky with their stoic eyes, as they contemplate their own Christmas dinner. The trees seem to be standing and shivering together, hugging bare limbs and grumbling about the cold. On this day more than any other, the Cistercians marvel at the hand of God in the Tipperary countryside.

Joy to the world

At morning Mass in the monastery there is a special feeling. Children prepare to worship who the night before were bursting with impatience, and had resolved to stay awake all night, to sneak a peep through the bannister, to catch a glimpse of Santa's red cloak. Then when sleep had defeated them they rushed downstairs, drawn as if by a magnet to the place under the Christmas tree, where hopefully Santa Claus had neatly piled their presents. Competition was intense as to who was to be the first to make the discovery, to shriek out, "He came, He came!" the excitement transmitting like electricity; their shining faces a fitting reward to the idea of Santa. Then the presents are pulled out and examined with squeaks of delight and excitement, muffled as far as possible to let any sleeping parents have a snooze. This is a time of mystery, and that spirit is carried in to their seasonal worship.

At Mass the priest wears his best gold and white robes. The pungent scent of greenery mingles with the waxy smell of burning candles. The final candle in the advent wreath is lit ceremoniously. So many images of Christ are etched in light, the silver of frost and moonlight, the shining Star of Bethlehem guarding the Magi and the radiance of the lighted candles. The candles quietly complemented the elation of the Gospel.

The Cistercians also read the nativity narratives story of how the angel spoke to the shepherds on the hillside and reported that: "They went in haste and found Mary and Joseph." Looking back now they wonder if that was the first Christmas rush!

In the congregation many are enthralled by the idea of angels. The pictures they have of angels are of creatures robed in white with outspread wings, kindly smiles and celestial vision. Angels are always good but essentially heavenly. The worshippers like them because they form a tenuous connection between the unseen worlds and signify the greatest of mysteries, humankind's passage through time.

When the liturgy is finished the congregation head home to prepare roaring fires which will provide leaping flames, dancing shadows and a rosy glow. After Christmas Mass the atmosphere is as Dickensian as Scrooge after the ghosts.

In Karl Rahner's magical phrase, Christmas is a time when "grace is in the air". Christmas Day is the best reminder to us that the eternal life in which we pray to be resurrected has long begun in a stable in Bethlehem.

In their message on their 2017 Christmas card, the Cistercians capture the essence of Christmas by citing from the *First Sermon for Advent* of St Bernard of Clairvaux:

"Truly the day was already far spent and the evening drawing near; the sun of justice was already beginning to set, and its rays now gave diminished light and warmth to the earth. The light of the knowledge of God had grown feeble, and as sin increased, charity grew cold. Angels no longer appeared to men, no prophet raised his voice; it seemed as though, overcome by the great hardness and obstinacy of men, they had ceased to intervene in human affairs. Then it was that the Son of God said: 'Here am I'."

The Saviour's Day

As a boy the two highlights of the television year for me were the National Song Contest and the Eurovison Song Contest. They were the only two nights of the year that my sisters and I were allowed to stay up very late to see the end of the voting. The stand out moment for me was seeing Abba for the first time as they romped home in the Eurovision final in Brighton with Waterloo.

The previous year though I had become a Cliff Richard fan. Some years earlier he had been the hottest of favourites to win the Eurovision with his party anthem 'Congratulations'. He lost. What struck me as strange though was that he was beaten by a Spanish song that seemed to consist of nothing but the singer singing 'La, La, La'. It might not have been a case for Amnesty International, but to my primary school mind it seemed a very serious injustice.

Then five years later Cliff had a second go at Eurovision with the song 'Power to All Our Friends'. Again he was favourite. He lost a second time. It may have been a sympathy thing rather than an act of musical admiration but that's when I became a fan. Once I started writing I decided to try and get an interview with him. To my surprise he quickly agreed to my request.

In recent years for many people Christmas and Cliff Richard have become synonymous. This is because Cliff's smash Christmas songs such as 'Mistletoe and Wine' and 'Saviour's Day' have become part of the furniture of our lives each December. When I met with Cliff just before Christmas in 1990 I wondered why he released so many Christmas songs.

"I just love Christmas. I love everything about it, the tree, the holly, the exchange of gifts and going to the midnight service in my local church. But above all I just love the spirit it creates every year, when for a few days people are nice to each other. I see it when I'm driving. Normally people won't give you the chance to get your car on to the main road but for those magic days everyone is incredibly kind," he said.

As someone who in recent years has experienced 'fake news' up close and personal, Cliff is evangelistic about what constitutes the Good News.

"Of course the 25th of December is special because we also celebrate the greatest Christmas gift of all time. Little things do mean a lot. As we prepare for Christmas we remember that God has showered us with gifts - none more so than when he sent his only Son. Those gifts come with a challenge. Christianity is not about occasional gestures of charity but about going the second mile, about making choices which involve inconvenience, discomfort and pain.

"The birth of Jesus offered a new beginning to the world, a new way of life. In this special season we are called again to take up Jesus' invitation to make a new beginning. The heart of this invitation is love because through love alone that we please God and our main challenge is to acquire it. Jesus came on earth to love and be loved - to win love for our love. The Christian life is an exchange of love - the love we receive and the love we give God," Cliff said.

I was expecting to meet a 'star' but instead I met a man who seemed unconcerned about celebrity, but instead was more concerned about living out his faith and being true to himself.

For all our claims to tolerance, pluralism and liberal values the phrase 'born again Christian' continues to attract derisory remarks and condescending laughs. Someone who claims to be 'born again' is immediately written off as a way-out, eccentric category of Christian, at least in certain quarters. Yet Cliff celebrates the term.

"As St Paul clearly shows in the second letter to the Corinthians, nothing could be further from the truth. 'Therefore, if anyone is in Christ, he is a new creation, the old has gone, the new has come.' If further evidence is needed, Jesus himself boldly declared: 'I tell you the truth, no one can see the Kingdom of God unless he is born again.' According to Jesus, rebirth is not an optional extra, but an essential part of Christianity: no rebirth - no Christian life for anybody," he said.

Cliff is a massive tennis fan and so I was not surprised to hear him using sporting metaphors.

"However, this new birth brings new responsibilities and difficulties. The Bible can never be accused of misleading advertising because the Christian is portrayed as someone who is active, tough, hard-working and dedicated. As we read in the second letter of Timothy, there's the soldier who in war must be disciplined, obedient and courageous; the farmer who toils long hours and never has the luxury of a day off, and the athlete who pushes his body to the limit to maintain peak fitness and whose sights are fixed exclusively on winning the race," he said.

"Christmas is an ideal time to be reborn in Christ. This is not to take out some kind of salvation insurance policy but to embrace a challenge of unconditional love that is terrifying in its demands. Christ is our saviour, certainly, but he is also Lord and, unless we accept him in both roles, we are not reborn and we don't receive him at all."

Cliff sees Christmas as a special time to spread the good news of Christianity.

"We often use words very casually. What do we really mean, when we speak of love, truth or beauty? It is easy to say that other four letter word, 'love', as thousands of pop songs and romantic novels have shown but it is much more difficult to practice it.'

"Love is at the very heart of the Christian life. After all, as we find in the first letter of St John, love is even God's definition. Christians are not simply God's possessions, but in a sense God's partners in loving," Cliff said.

"I like to think also that especially at Christmas, with those for whom there is no one to share their rooms is Jesus. The sad reality is that life is difficult for many people. The message of Christmas is that Christ is made flesh not in the unreal beauty of the Christmas card, but in the mess that is our world. For those of us who claim to be Christian, Christ is made flesh in our neighbours.

"Few of us have the power to change the world but this Christmas we can all do something, albeit something small, to improve life for our neighbour. Today the depth of our commitment to Christ is guaged by the extent to which we love our neighbour," he said.

Cliff, though, is keen to set Christmas in a wider context.

"It was Jesus who came and brought our understanding of love to new heights. There are many ways of looking at the life of Christ. The way I like to think of his life is as a great drama, in which Christ himself is the central character, and all the people he meets have supporting roles. It is a love that enriches others, but which in the end cost Christ his own life. The Christmas story is meaningless in isolation from Easter. Love is unconditional, total commitment. Christ showed the ultimate act of love, by giving up his life on that wooden cross. One of the clearest messages of Jesus' life is that we speak the language of love much more eloquently with our actions than with our words.'

Cliff emphasised the fact that Christmas was the point of demarcation between the old and the new, and he spoke about his faith with the passion of a medieval martyr.

"One of the key messages of Christmas, which I celebrate anew each year is: The old is past, there is a new beginning. Sometimes we fear to take a new step, to speak a new word. Change is all around us and our task is to build a better tomorrow."

Cliff was very engaged by every question he was asked and keen to answer each query with complete candour. He is very keen on the symbolism of Christmas.

"Another thing that fascinates me is that Christmas is a time of apparent contradictions. A king is born as a commoner. A birth signals the death of the old regime. Strength is clothed in weakness. Riches are disguised as poverty. Yet the real message of Christmas is very simple – 'God so loved the world that He sent His only son'.

"The human capacity to take control of difficult situations is remarkable. In our complex world to be in control is everything. Yet the paradox of Christianity is that the more we let go, the more we receive, because God's action is more effective in our lives," Cliff said.

For Cliff, Christmas is the ultimate contradiction – but in a positive way.

"God was born as a baby to highlight that in our weakness we will find strength to live the Christian life. If we were strong enough to do everything ourselves we would not have needed Jesus in the first place. Our earthly life is not a long examination paper where we earn salvation through our own feeble efforts, but a chance to let God's love explode within us."

The Chistmas Presence

Yes, they know its Christmas

In 1672, in Cologne, Germany, the choirmaster at the local church, wishing to remedy the noise caused by children during the Christmas service, asked a local candy maker for some sweet sticks for them. In order to justify the practice of giving candy canes to children during Mass, he asked the candy maker to add a crook to the top of each stick, which would help children remember the shepherds who paid a visit to the baby Jesus. The practice spread to America and beyond.

Something's cooking in the kitchen

Culinary innovation was not a feature of my childhood. Then, when I was 18, my mother caused a major shock when she produced Brussel sprouts for Christmas dinner. It was the first time any of us had ever seen them. My grandfather looked at them for a long time and poked them around his plate for what seemed like an eternity with a disdainful look on his face. We waited his verdict with bated breath. Eventually he asked, "Who made balls of the cabbage?"

The following year we had another surprise when my mother introduced us to mince pies. My grandfather despised them. He insisted on calling them, "mice pies'.

Christmas is a time for....

Christmas is a time for celebration,
to spread love, to offer friendship,
for reconciliation.

Christmas is a time for reflection,
to illuminate hope, to alleviate suffering,
for communication.

Christmas is a time for happiness,
to wash away sorrow, to embrace a neighbour, f
or tenderness.

Christmas is a time for giving,
to accept gifts, to give thanks,
for living.

Christmas is a time to cast differences aside,
to pardon transgressions, to forget grievances,
to abandon foolish pride.

Christmas is a time to remember,
all the children of God
who are suffering in December.

(Anon)

SECTION B:

BEAUTIFUL THOUGHTS FOR YOUNGER MINDS

Introduction

It is often said that the biggest gift someone can give a child is the gift of reading. I wanted this book to have a special section which might appeal to younger readers – though I would like to think it may also be of interest to the young at heart.

Often times we underestimate children. They, more than any other group, have beautiful minds untainted by cynicism or disillusionment. So why then should they not be exposed to beautiful thoughts?

I would like to think this book is a gift that could be shared across the generations. As a child my favourite time of the year was Christmas. To this day Christmas continues to awaken the child within me. So I include two Christmas stories which may be of particular interest to the young – but I hope might capture the Christmas Presence for the more mature as well. They will hopefully appeal to those who in the wonderful words of Bob Dylan remain 'forever young'.

The Reindeer Who Saved Christmas

Revenge of the Easter Bunny

The Easter Bunny was really, really angry. In fact she had never been madder in all her life. And when she was angry she wasn't a pretty sight.

She had just finished reading a special issue of Celebrity Magazine. For the first time in its history, Celebrity had devoted its entire issue to just one person: Santa Claus. There was a big spread on Santa and Mrs Claus at home in the North Pole; Santa with his reindeers and his elves; Santa's favourite music, books, television programmes; and interviews celebrities like Ed Sheeran and Katy Perry talking about why Santa was magic.

Hello had always been the Easter Bunny's favourite magazine. But as she tore her copy into a thousand little pieces she swore that she would never, ever buy it again.

.Last month, for the 20th year in a row, the magazine had presented the People's Hero Award to Santa. They had counted down the all-time top thousand people's champions. And what number was the Easter Bunny on that list? Why, she wasn't mentioned at all! What an insult. How could she be less important than pop singers, footballers and actors? She had never felt so hurt.

Since Easter, she had thought about nothing but appearing on *Hello*'s list. In her heart of hearts she wanted to beat Santa Claus to number one, though she would never have admitted that to any of her bunny friends. But she wanted to win, and that meant other people had to lose.

Normally the Easter Bunny was the nicest and most gentle creature you could ever meet. But if she ever lost her temper, you didn't want to be near her. It was like watching a volcano explode!

After hours and hours of thinking of plans to get to the top of that list, at last, she got an idea. She shouted out, "I've got it! I've got the perfect plan. I'm going to kidnap Santa Claus and cancel Christmas."

Nightmare on Halloween

"This is going to be the best Christmas ever," said Santa to Mrs Claus as he warmed his bum beside a blazing log fire.

"Why do you say that, my love?" asked Mrs Claus in a curious voice.

"I have something up my sleeve," replied Santa.

"Really. What exactly, pet?" asked Mrs Claus, getting a bit excited.

"My arm!" said Santa. He began to roar laughing. Santa had the most wonderful laugh in all the land.

Mrs Claus laughed at his answer. Like her husband, she

had a great sense of humour. Last Christmas Santa caught a chill while delivering all the toys and got a terrible pain in his ear. He had to go into the local hospital for a minor ear operation. On the first of January Mrs Claus visited her husband in the hospital and presented him with a colourful card which read: 'Happy New Ear's Day'.

Since then Santa had taken things easy, but today was Halloween. It was one of his favourite days in all the year. He always held a big party in his house for all his helpers. Tomorrow they would start preparing for Christmas and everyone would work all day, every day to make sure every child in the world got their presents on Christmas morning. Letters from boys and girls all the world over had to be read, lists had to be prepared and toys had to be wrapped. Today was the last day for Santa to let his hair and beard down until he had a late, late Christmas dinner on Christmas Day when all the toys were safely delivered and children everywhere were happy.

That Halloween morning, Rudolph the Red-Nosed Reindeer and his children had come to put up the Christmas decorations in Santa's house. Rudolph had nine children: seven boys and twin daughters. Cards, showing people walking about snowy landscapes, decorated the walls. On the top of the big Christmas tree was a tin foil star. There were little silver balls, lights like tiny stars and pale-coloured tinsel threaded among the tree's branches. Round the bottom were boxes of presents done up in pretty paper tied with red ribbon.

Although the lights were off, the crickle-crackle log fire provided leaping flames, dancing shadows and a rosy glow. Everything looked lovely. Then, disaster! Rudolph's youngest son, Rinky Ray, knocked over the Christmas tree.

Nobody was surprised. Rinky Ray was a walking disaster. He was a dreamer and usually didn't pay much attention to what he was doing or where he was going. He often got lost on the way to reindeer school.

Rudolph always had a soft spot for his youngest son even though he caused a lot of problems. Rinky Ray was different from all Rudolph's other children because he didn't have a shiny, red nose. He had a tiny, tiny white nose. He would have loved to have even a red freckle on it, but it was as white as snow. Poor Rinky Ray had an awful time at school because the other reindeer were always teasing him about his nose. They called him 'No Nose'. A few times each day they even sang a song about him:

> *Rinky Ray the white nose reindeer*
> *hasn't a very shiny nose*
> *and if you ever saw it*
> *you'd never say it glows.*
> *Rinky Ray with your nose so white*
> *you'll never join Santa's sleigh on Christmas night.*

There was a big crash as the tree smashed onto the floor. Everybody went very quiet for a minute and then they all looked at Rinky Ray. Rinky Ray just looked down at his tiny hooves, with tears trickling down his cheeks.

"No harm done," said Santa Claus in a soft, kind voice..

"I'm really sorry Santa. I'm really sorry Dad."

"I know you are son," said Rudolph, "but why don't you go out and play while we tidy up the mess and get everything back the way it was. I'll call you in when we've finished. Don't worry. Nobody's cross with you. Isn't that right Santa?"

"Of course. I know it was an accident. It could happen to anyone," said Santa. He hated to see anyone crying.

Can I tell you a really big secret? Santa cries a lot himself. He's such a big softie, he cries when he watches sad movies. Don't tell anybody. He cried a bucket full of tears when he saw *The Lion King*. He even cried when he watched *Shrek*!

So Rinky Ray dried up his tears and went out to play. The first snow of winter had fallen that morning. "I've got a great idea. I'll make a snowman. It'll be a lovely surprise for my brothers and sisters," thought Rinky Ray. He looked around to see where the snow was thickest. The thickest snow was beside the warehouse. Rinky Ray peeked in at it. That morning one million Harry Potter books had been delivered and they were all piled up in a book mountain that seemed as big as the tower of London. Looking at the books, Rinky Ray said to himself, "A lot of children will be very, very happy this Christmas," with a big smile on his face.

Slowly and carefully Rinky Ray started to build a snowman. Rinky Ray was really proud of himself when he had finished. He had never seen a nicer snowman. The problem was it was just starting to rain. The rain would melt the snowman. "How can I save him?", wondered Rinky Ray to himself. A lot of the other reindeers didn't realise that Rinky Ray was very bright. So when he really put his mind to something he could do great things.

Then he got a brainwave. He picked up the snowman and stored him in the big freezer in the warehouse. That would keep the snowman nice and cold. He would take him out first thing tomorrow morning and surprise his siblings then.

As Rinky Ray was so busy with his snowman, he didn't take any notice of what was happening up at Santa's house. He heard a lot of noise but he ignored it. An hour later he would be very, very sorry he didn't pay attention.

After Rinky Ray had gone outside, Santa's Halloween party continued. Santa was just in the middle of his fourth muffin and third glass of milk when the doorbell rang.

"That's very strange," said Santa to Mrs Claus. "I'm not expecting anyone."

Rudolph was putting up some decorations in the hall so he answered the door. He was very surprised to see the Easter Bunny at the door.

"I thought you only appeared at Easter. Come on in," said Rudolph.

Santa got up from his armchair. It was his first time meeting the Easter Bunny and he was very surprised to see her in the North Pole. Before he could say anything, the Easter Bunny said, "Santa Claus, it's a great honour to meet the most famous man in the whole world and the only person that everybody loves."

Santa Claus gave one of his famous, ho, ho, ho's as he welcomed the Easter Bunny into his home. Then the Easter Bunny spoke again.

"I've brought you a gift Santa. I made three cakes for you and all your helpers and I want everyone to have a slice now."

"You're so kind. I can't believe you came all this way to bring us some cake. You must be the nicest creature in the world. Those cakes look delicious. It was very sweet of you to ice them and decorate them with pictures of me. Everyone, come and have a slice of the Easter Bunny's cake."

Mrs Claus, the elves, Rudolph and all the reindeer gathered around and took a slice of cake each. But hard as he tried, Santa couldn't get the Easter Bunny to have a slice of one of her own cakes. Santa was too nice to say anything, but he didn't like her cake. There was something funny about the taste. As he looked around, he realized that the others weren't enjoyed the taste, either, but were too polite to say anything.

After a few minutes Santa started yawning. Then Mrs Claus began to yawn. Suddenly everyone in the room was yawning except the Easter Bunny.

"I'm sooo sorry. I'm--I'm just going to have a little snooze," said Santa Claus in a very tired voice. Soon Santa was fast asleep and snoring loudly.

Within a few minutes everyone in the room was fast asleep. Except the Easter Bunny. She was rubbing her hands with glee. She had put a sleeping drug into her cakes and everyone who tasted her cakes was now in a deep sleep.

The Easter Bunny made a quick call on her mobile phone. A few minutes later there was a screeching noise outside Santa's house. A big truck pulled up outside. A bunch of her bunny friends jumped out and helped her load hide Santa and his friends into the car, then they screeched away to a secret destination.

Meanwhile, Rinky Ray had just finished storing his snowman in the freezer and was feeling hungry. He was thinking of the big press full of carrots that Santa kept in his kitchen. By now heavy showers of icy rain were sweeping over the North Pole, carried by gusts of bitter wind. The evening had become dark and dreary.

As he walked up to the house, Rinky Ray peeked in through the windows and saw there was nobody in the living room. Then he peeked through the kitchen window, but again there was no one to be seen.

"I know what's happening," Rinky Ray thought to himself. "Santa's playing a trick on me." Rinky Ray tiptoed into Santa's house. He kept expecting Santa and his helpers to jump out of the wardrobes and say "Surprise!". But nothing happened.

Then Rinky Ray saw a letter on the kitchen table. He rushed over to read it. He could not believe what he read. It said:

I've kidnapped Santa Claus and all his helpers. If anybody comes looking for him, something dreadful will happen. I'll let him and his helpers out at Easter if everyone behaves themselves. Whatever you do, make sure nobody comes searching for him. If you do you will be very, very sorry.

Rinky Ray gulped as he re-read the last line: *Christmas is Cancelled*

Rinky Ray's tummy ached, his head hurt, and his throat felt scratchy. He let out a horrible sound. He would have to go out into the snow to try and find his family, friends and Santa Claus.

The chill of the late afternoon made Rinky Ray shiver. The winter that year had been cold and stormy so far. Normally, on a late winter afternoon with darkness due and snow-clouds threatening, Rinky Ray would have not been allowed out. But this was no time to stay inside. He knew that he had to find answers. Where was everybody?

"It's so cold," said Rinky Ray to himself. His teeth were chattering in the icy air. He walked towards the forest through the already ankle-deep snow. Rinky Ray had never known such cold. He called out everyone's name as he walked, but no one replied.

Darkness had fallen like an angry giant. Thankfully the white-nosed reindeer had brought a torch with him. There would be more snow within the hour. Rinky Ray could do no more searching that night. He headed back for Santa's house. The warm house awaited him like a sanctuary. As soon as he got inside Rinky Ray fell on the floor with exhaustion. Just before he fell into a deep sleep, a tiny tear toppled down his cheek. He realised that only he could save Christmas.

But how could he possibly do it on his own?

The Terrible Truth

After Christmas every year Santa and Mrs Claus go to Florida for two months for some sun and relaxation. On the day after he returns from his holidays Santa throws a big party for all who helped to make his Christmas journey such a great success. The next day though, work starts for the following Christmas. Santa does like to try and do things better each year. The first step is to look back and see could he improve on what happened during the last Christmas Eve.

To help him do this he makes a video of Christmas Eve in his factory to see if he could improve things and his first job in March is to watch the video. Why am I telling you this? Because Santa never leaves anything to chance. To make sure the video recording equipment is working properly he always tests it out by recording his Halloween party. And that was Rinky Ray's brainwave the next morning. He would be able to find out who kidnapped Santa and his helpers by checking the video.

Rinky Ray ran up to the audio-visual room and watched the video. Outside the heavy rain and gusting wind crashed against the windows. The dark, sickly sky closed in. He smiled at first while watching the party, until he reached the bit when he knocked down the Christmas tree. He fast-forwarded past that bit a until he saw the Easter Bunny arriving.

He recognised her almost immediately. She was tall and thin. Her appearance was always slightly untidy, but in the video she looked so rumpled that Rinky Ray hardly recognized her. Her face was more wrinkled and looked almost grey. She was frowning, her once-dark hair was silver now, and her ice-blue eyes were the angriest Rinky Ray had ever seen.

He had to find a way of freeing Santa and his helpers. He couldn't let this scary person take his friends and family away. But how could one young reindeer take on the Easter Bunny ? Things looked hopeless. He had never felt so miserable.

The Land of Make-believe

Can I tell you one last secret? The Easter Bunny gets very forgetful when she gets excited.

She forgot that she had a hole in her bag, and when she kidnapped Santa and his friends, out of her bag were spilling the little Easter eggs she kept with her.

As she rode on her motorbike to Land of Make-believe she left a trail of Easter eggs all the way there. Rinky Ray could not believe his luck when he discovered them outside. All he had to do was to follow the trail of Easter Eggs and he would arrive safely at the secret hideaway.

When he finally got to the Land of Make-believe he discovered that the Easter Bunny lived in a big house made of chocolate. It looked lovely and Rinky Ray was tempted to see if it tasted delicious, too, but decided he should set Santa and his friends free first. He looked in the window and there was the Easter Bunny, fast asleep in her chair. In the corner were poor Santa Claus and the rest of his friends tied up and looking miserable. Rinky Ray crept softly through the door and smiled at his old friend, Santa Claus. Santa Claus' eyes opened wide with surprise and delight. After untying everyone, they all tiptoed quietly out the door. That evening they were all safely home in the North Pole.

After he had his lovely turkey dinner, followed by a glass of milk and one, actually two, mince pies, Santa told

Rinky Ray that as a thank you for saving the day, Rinky Ray could be his special helper on Christmas Eve. Rinky Ray squealed with delight. He had saved the day and kept Christmas from being cancelled.

The Christmas Guest

That Christmas Eve Santa Claus had a big surprise for Rinky Ray. Since he had saved Christmas for all the children of the world, Rinky Ray was Santa's special helper, helping him deliver presents to girls and boys all over the world.

When they got to Dublin, Rinky Ray took a minute to watch Claire Butler sleeping soundly. The beautiful Christmas stocking that her mother Siobhan had lovingly placed at the foot of her bed was full of the Christmas presents Santa had left for her.

A big smile grew on Rinky Ray's face.

Christmas really was the most wonderful time of the year.

The Doctor Who Could Not See

Once upon a time, about two thousand years ago, there lived a girl called Catherine. She was a shy eight-year-old who was unable to find evil in others. Although her nose was a little lumpy, her teeth were crooked and her lips were paper thin, she had a real beauty to her. She was partially blind from birth and went everywhere with her guidedog, JoJo.

Most days she looked slightly rumpled. Her hair was never neat and she generally looked a bit untidy. Her room was such a mess she had to wipe her shoes after leaving it. She sometimes spoke slowly and then used her hands to help find and say the right words. When she listened, she played with her long, jet-black hair and often seemed to be biting a fingernail.

She was a dreamer and usually didn't pay much attention to what she was doing or where she was going. She often got lost on the way to school. Her father said that she had a brain the size of a pea, but that her heart was bigger than a horse.

Catherine had a dream. She believed that one day she would become a great doctor. Her mother had died after her foot got an infection and Catherine wanted to cure people, especially those poor people with sore feet. Although everyone laughed at her when she told them about her dream, she knew in her heart and soul that one day the dream would come true.

On this day though Catherine was in a state of total panic. That morning she had been carrying home a big bowl of water. It was much too heavy really for an eight-year-old like herself. She loved her father so much that she went to bring him some refreshing water from the well, so that he could have a nice drink when his work was finished.

She had almost made the mile and a half home when she lost her balance and the bowl crashed onto the ground, smashing into a hundred tiny pieces. She knew immediately that this meant big, big trouble from her father.

Catherine's Dad had a terrible temper. She hated it when he was in bad mood.

Most of the time he was very nice and kind, but when he got angry he was really, really angry, and it wasn't a pretty sight.

He was a tall, thin man with long hands. He lived with Catherine in a lonely house on the side of a mountain by a green grass track which led to the tiny village of Whitepark.

But Catherine's dad was a sad man. His wife had died when Catherine was five.

Catherine was a real Daddy's girl. Her father got up an hour before her to milk their one cow. There he was, a shoe-maker, staying up half the night making shoes so there would be enough money for everything his daughter needed but also doing the washing, matching Catherine's socks, remembering her birthday, checking her home-work, peeling potatoes, cleaning shoes and telling bedtime stories. Some men had it all, but he had to do it all. Even on the most busy weeks he brought Catherine to church every Sunday.

In the morning he put a grain of sugar on Catherine's tongue. He thought this would help Catherine say nothing but nice, sweet words. At night he would put a grain of sugar on her head so that she would have sweet dreams. Then he put a grain of sugar on her ears so that the last thing she would hear before she went to sleep and the first thing she would hear when she woke up was something nice.

One day he brought her for a walk in the country. Suddenly Catherine shouted, "Daddy, Daddy, stop! stop! There's a kitten back there on the side of the road!"

Catherine's Dad said, "So there's a kitten on the side of the road. We're out for a walk."

"But, Daddy, you must stop and pick it up."

"I don't have to stop and pick it up."

"But, Daddy, if you don't it will die."

"Well, then it will have to die. We don't have room for another animal. We already have a dog at our house and a cow in our barn. No more animals."

"But, Daddy, are you just going to let it die?"

"Be, quiet, Catherine. We're just going to have a nice walk."

"I never thought my Daddy would be so mean and cruel as to let a kitten die."

At that moment Catherine's Dad turned around and returned to the spot at the side of the road. He bent down to pick up the kitten. The poor creature was just skin and bones but when Catherine's Dad reached down to pick it up with its last energy the kitten bared his teeth and claw. "Ssst! Sssst!" said the cat. Catherine's Dad picked up the kitten and brought it back to the car and said "Catherine, don't touch it. It's probably full of disease."

When they got home they gave the kitten several baths, about a pint of milk, and Catherine begged, "Can we let it stay in the house just tonight? Tomorrow we'll fix a place in the shed." Her father said, "Okay."

Catherine watched quietly in the corner as her father fixed a comfortable bed, fit for a prince.

Catherine loved her father very much, because he was such a good man. He was also very kind and gentle. These dark, cold weeks of winter were his busiest time of the year. As the bad weather came and with the rain dripping through the holes in the roof and the wind howling through many of the many gaps in the walls he needed money badly. He worked 18 hours a day, seven days a week, because he had a big contract to make new boots for all the soldiers in the king's army.

Most times Catherine's dad was not angry when Catherine did something wrong, but she knew that her Dad would not be happy when he saw the broken bowl. Her Mum had given him that bowl for his birthday and it was something he always treasured. Now Catherine had broken it. Her Dad would be so angry and would shout at her very loudly. He was the nicest and most gentle creature you could ever meet, but if he ever lost his temper you didn't want to be near him. It was like watching a volcano explode. You just wanted to get as far away as fast as possible. Heaven help you if you got in his way. He would be home soon. What, oh what, could she do? Catherine was in a state of total panic.

Catherine decided she would run away with JoJo. She ran and ran until she got very tired. By now it was very dark. They reached the nearby small town of Bethlehem which, unusually, was full of people. Catherine was scared by all the noise and started to cry. A kindly old shopkeeper saw her and gave her some apples and oranges. Catherine was overjoyed and went to find a quiet place to enjoy this feast.

Just as she was sitting down outside a stable, she heard some shadowy figures come out from the darkness. Catherine was upset when she heard the woman moaning in pain and holding her stomach. "That poor creature must be very hungry," thought Catherine. She brought over all the apples and oranges to the couple. They thanked her warmly and then the man helped the woman into the stable and laid her down on a bed of straw.

Suddenly Catherine felt a great sense of peace sweep over her and she decided she would return home with JoJo. On her way she heard a man say there was a great star in the east. She remembered that her teacher had told her that there was a promise that a star would come from the East to guide the three wise men in search of a saviour. The only problem was that they couldn't find three wise men in all the East, so three wise women would come instead.

She was half-way home when she met three beautiful women with dark skin and wavy air, in magnificent robes on camels. They were carrying what looked like very expensive presents. "Young girl do you know where the new king was born tonight?" one asked. "I'm afraid I know nothing about that ladies but there was a lot going on in Bethlehem this evening."

"Please tell us what you saw," said one of the women. "My name is Ruth, by the way, and this is Roberta and Rachel."

While Catherine told them everything that had happened to her the three women listened very carefully. When she had finished Ruth asked, "I know you are very tired but would you be kind enough to take us to see that woman in the stable?"

"My mother told me never to talk to strangers, but you seem very nice so I will help you," replied Catherine.

Quick as a flash Ruth stretched out her long arm and pulled Catherine up beside her on her camel. The three camels took off at great speed with JoJo running behind them faster than he had ever run before.

By now it was hard to find their way. It was a dark night, as black as the ace of spades. Not a star was to be seen. It was bitterly cold. Catherine's breath was coming out on to the cold air like puffs of steam from a kettle. Snowflakes began to fall, timidly at first, then getting very strong as the shyness appeared to wear off them.

A few swirling snowflakes drifted onto her head. The camels guessed their way along the side of the road, and one stumbled and almost fell into a wet ditch. Only a cow lowing in a distant field shattered the spell of silence. The camels plodded up the pathway, through the thickening snow-storm, leaving big, deep footprints in the fresh snow.

Strangely Catherine still felt happy, though now the snow was making a white carpet on her hair. The whole sky seemed to be filled with dizzy, dancing snow. The blanket of white created a light that gave life to hedges and houses, so that night started to look like day.

As they passed by an empty school, a little robin was hopping on the window-sill in search of crumbs. The sticks on the ground were glittering with the night frost and the snow. In the fields cattle were huddling under creeping hedges, staring up at the snowy sky with their tired eyes. The trees seemed to be standing and shivering together, hugging bare limbs and grumbling about the cold. A few tattered leaves made a blanket on the frozen earth.

Catherine was a bit scared, but she was also thrilled. It was her first time on a camel. A short time later they reached the stable. For the moment the snow had stopped.

Even before they got to the door Catherine could hear a baby crying. "Where did that baby come from?" she thought to herself. A few shepherds were rushing in before them in a state of great excitement. Some of them were carrying armfuls of nice, clean straw.

Catherine walked in behind the women and stood beside one of the big shepherds. The stable was dirty, damp and very, very smelly. There were a lot of holes in the stable walls so a chilly wind was blowing through, giving Catherine the shivers. Lying in the corner was the woman Catherine had met earlier with a baby in her arms. Except she wasn't fat anymore. "How could anyone go from fat to thin so quickly?" Catherine thought to herself. The baby had no clothes on him and Catherine could hear the shepherds saying that it was a boy. The man she had given her apples and oranges to earlier was crying softly. Catherine had never heard of a man crying before. Yet he also had a smile on his face. How could anyone be crying and smiling at the one time? This was very odd.

The shepherds were standing with their mouths open and their hands in their pockets. They had no idea what to do.

The three women took control. They told the shepherds to stand back. Ruth pointed to two of the shepherds and in a strong voice said, "Get those cows out of here. Can't you see they shouldn't be in the same place as a baby?" The two shepherds did as they were told, as if they were little children. Catherine thought Ruth must be a teacher, she was so good at giving orders. The woman told Rachel that her name was Mary and that the man's name was Joseph.

Then the three women presented gifts to Mary. Roberta went first and she gave the new mother a basket of lovely soaps, oils and face-cloths as well as the tiniest clothes anybody had ever seen in Bethlehem. Roberta bathed Mary and her baby with some of them. When Mary and her baby were nice and clean she dressed the baby in some of his new clothes. As it was very cold in the stable she put on the cutest little woollen cap on his head and lovely little gloves on his tiny hands.

Next came Rachel and she presented Mary with a beautiful silk nightdress and dressing-gown. The nightdress had an amazing twirly design and the dressing-gown was covered in little stars. Rachel held the baby as Mary put on her new clothes. Catherine imagined she looked like a queen. All that was missing was a crown for her head. Rachel then took out a hairbrush and brushed Mary's long, black hair as if she was preparing her for a big party rather than to sit in a stable.

Finally, Ruth opened the wrapping paper off a bulky object. Mary's eyes nearly fell out of her head when Ruth calmly put a magnificent crib on the strawy floor and placed the baby in it and wrapped his blanket around him. She then gently left a book beside the baby who already had the most magical smile. It was a copy of the classic Jewish folktale - *The Adventures of Barry Totter.*

In whispery voices Mary and Joseph thanked the three women for their beautiful presents. Catherine felt bad that she had no gift for the baby. She quietly slipped outside with JoJo again leading her on the way. Nobody even noticed that she was gone.

Her father was a poor man and could not afford to buy anything like the presents the three women had bought for this new child. But Catherine did not worry. Young though she was, she knew that it was not the value of the gift that matters, but the spirit in which it is given. She went out to the woods and got a tiny holly tree and dug it up with her hands. It was a poor little thing without a single berry on it, but Catherine carried the offering to the stable.

When she walked back in the shepherds started laughing at her miserable-looking plant. Catherine was very sad when she heard them making little of her gift. She knelt down before the baby's crib and, in a shaking voice, she said, "Dear little child, I'm sorry I could not give you a beautiful present. The little holly tree was the best I could find, and I give it to you. I always give of my best."

As soon as Catherine had finished speaking a great hush fell upon the stable, for a wonderful thing had happened before their eyes. The colourless little holly tree was covered with a mass of glowing red berries.

It was the first Christmas miracle.

All the shepherds dropped on their knees beside Catherine and prayed like they had never prayed before.

Across the fields the houses glittered, the light from their candles shining brightly in the darkness. People walked to the church to give thanks for the birth of the new baby Jesus even though the snow was still falling.

Then the three women kissed Catherine on the cheeks and sent her home. As she left Ruth said, "You know that in thousands of years children all around the world will be talking about what happened tonight. Shopkeepers will sell cards about it. Gift shops will open to make presents about it. Bakeries will bake cakes to celebrate it. People will wonder about what really happened. But you were there in the stable, my darling. You are so lucky. That is probably the greatest gift anybody could ever get. Everyone who missed tonight in Bethlehem has really missed out.

"Go home my child and remember what you have seen here. Never forget that when you give to God with a good heart, He will accept your gift gladly, and, no matter how poor it may be, the touch of His hand will enrich and beautify it."

The next morning the strangest thing happened. When Catherine woke up she could see clearly. She smiled because she knew she had been given a great gift from God to help others.

Catherine grew up to be an amazing and exceptional woman. She became the greatest surgeon in all the land and every day people came to visit her in the hospital. Everybody called her 'the woman with the magic hands' and every day she performed little miracles by healing people's sore feet. With her little miracles, she made each day like Christmas.

Parting Thoughts

Just A Thought

....

"For Christ plays in ten thousand places,
Lovely in limbs,
And lovely in eyes not his."
(Gerard Manley Hopkins)

Who Are You?

....

You are a unique manifestation of the love of God.

The Last Words

....

"Our lives begin to end the day we become silent about the
things that matter . . . . In the End, we will remember not
the words of our enemies, but the silence of our friends."
(Martin Luther King Jr)

"We speak when we do not speak. We act when we do not act."
(Dietrich Bonhoeffer)

The Very Last Word

....

"Self-esteem is seeing yourself as God sees you."
(Patricia Seery)

Afterword

For Gareth O'Callaghan

You Still Have Hope

If you can look at the sunset and smile,
then you still have hope.

If you can find beauty in the colours of a small flower,
then you still have hope.

If you can find pleasure in the movement of a butterfly,
then you still have hope.

If the smile of a child can still warm your heart,
then you still have hope.

If you can see the good in other people,
then you still have hope.

If the rain breaking on a roof top can still lull you to sleep,
then you still have hope.

If the sight of a rainbow still makes you stop and stare in
wonder,
then you still have hope.

If the soft fur of a favoured pet still feels pleasant under
your fingertips,
then you still have hope.

If you meet new people with a trace of excitement
and optimism,
then you still have hope.

If you give people the benefit of a doubt,
then you still have hope.

If you still offer your hand in friendship to others that
have touched your life,
then you still have hope.

If receiving an unexpected card
or letter still brings a pleasant surprise,
then you still have hope.

If the suffering of others still fills you
with pain and frustration,
then you still have hope.

If you refuse to let a friendship die,
or accept that it must end,
then you still have hope.

If you look forward to a time or place of quiet and reflection,
then you still have hope.

If you still buy the ornaments,
put up the Christmas tree or cook the supper,
then you still have hope.

If you can look to the past and smile,
then you still have hope.

If, when faced with the bad,
when told everything is futile,
you can still look up and end the conversation with the
phrase..."yeah...BUT,"
then you still have hope.

Hope is such a marvelous thing.

It bends, it twists, it sometimes hides,
but rarely does it break.
It sustains us when nothing else can.
It gives us reason to continue and courage to move ahead,
when we tell ourselves we'd rather give in.
Hope puts a smile on our face.

when the heart cannot manage.
Hope puts our feet on the path.

when our eyes cannot see it.
Hope moves us to act.

when our souls are confused of the direction.
Hope is a wonderful thing,

something to be cherished and nurtured,
and something that will refresh us in return.
And it can be found in each of us,
and it can bring light into the darkest of places.

NEVER LOSE HOPE!

(Anon)